PUFFIN BOOKS

A CHANCE CHILD

Into the Place, a no man's land of weeds, litter, crushed and broken things, emerges a ragged, shivering child. He doesn't seem to know much, except that he must move on. So he makes his way down to the canal – and there he acquires a name, and a boat to travel on.

Two more children follow after Creep, searching for him – but they have no boat and not much chance of finding a small lost boy. Pauline gives up and goes home, but Christopher can't bear the thought of home without Creep. Then he finds a clue – Creep's name scratched crookedly on the side of a bridge! But it is puzzling as much as heartening. The letters are encrusted with moss and lichen, and partly nibbled away by grooves that horses' tow ropes have worn. They had been carved a hundred and fifty years ago!

Creep's journey along the waterway takes him through a strange dreamlike landscape where green fields and hills are interspersed with furnaces and smoky factories. Here, men, women and children labour painfully for a meagre wage. Creep, the outsider, is slowly drawn into this world, as he befriends first Tom the collier, then Blackie the nailer. And we too are drawn into a haunting, poignant past, powerfully created by one of our finest writers of historical fiction.

Jill Paton Walsh was brought up in London and read English at Oxford University. She is married with three children.

JILL PATON WALSH

◆

A Chance Child

◆ ◆ ◆ ◆ ◆ ◆ ◆ ◆
◆ ◆ ◆ ◆

PUFFIN BOOKS

Puffin Books, Penguin Books Ltd, Harmondsworth, Middlesex, England
Viking Penguin Inc., 40 West 23rd Street, New York, New York 10010, U.S.A.
Penguin Books Australia Ltd, Ringwood, Victoria, Australia
Penguin Books Canada Limited, 2801 John Street, Markham, Ontario, Canada L3R 1B4
Penguin Books (N.Z.) Ltd, 182–190 Wairau Road, Auckland 10, New Zealand

—

First published by Macmillan London Ltd 1978
Published in Puffin Books 1985
Reprinted 1987

—

—

Made and printed in Great Britain by
Richard Clay (The Chaucer Press) Ltd,
Bungay, Suffolk

To: Robert Blincoe, poor-house apprentice; Thomas Moorhouse, aged nine, a collier; Margaret Leveston, aged 6, a coal bearer; Witness No 96, aged sixteen as far as he could guess, a nailer; Jacob Ball, aged 12, a dish mould runner; Joseph Badder, spinner, who was sorry to beat little children; Joseph Hebergam, a worsted spinner from seven years old, whose mother wept to see him grow crooked; William Kershaw, aged 8, a "piecener" whose mother beat his master over the head with a billy-roller; Emanual Lovekin, mining butty, who learned to read and write while lying injured; and many others whose names and stories I have made use of in this book in one way or another, and to innumerable others like them.

The landscape of this book is fantasy, and yet for every place described in it, some such place exists somewhere.

1

Rain had been falling on the cardboard box for nearly an hour when it began to move. The box was lying on a dump, with other abandoned and useless things. Above it a grey sky oozed a misty rain of fine droplets that gradually moistened the surface of everything beneath, coating it all with a slick of wetness. The letters on the cardboard box, red stencil, saying SURPLUS TO REQUIREMENTS were quickly blurred. Then, as more rain fell, the card became sodden and began to disintegrate into a pale brown slime. And though everything else bore its wetting patiently, unmoved by the fall of rain, the box wriggled, shuddered, shifted as it soaked through.

At last there was a sudden convulsive movement from within the wilting cardboard, and out of it crept a ragged and shivering child.

The child crouched beside the box, its thin arms hugged around its ribs, and looked about, with a bird-like, darting glance. It had bright brown gimlet eyes, screwed up against the grey rainlight. It seemed to find nothing cheerful in its surroundings. A sigh as large as its body suddenly shook its frame. Then it stood up, tottering a little on thin, stick-bone legs, and began to weave to and fro, traversing the Place, up mounds and down pits, while the rain beat lightly and steadily down.

The Place was pitted and mounded. Not with earth, though on the rotted-down surface, here and there, brave dirty weeds had taken precarious root. Some of the mounds were of rubbish, reeking of fermentation, of corruption; more were of things. Crushed, broken, mangled, rusting and perishing things—old cars, iron mechanisms, squashed drums lay in such confusion that the eye refused to sort them. Perhaps the pits were something, perhaps they were only the absence of mounds; they appeared, steep and deep though some of them were, not to reach down as far as native earth. Stone and gravel were embedded in their floors, and twisted and broken rails threaded through the greasy glint of foul puddles lying down there.

First the child climbed into the rusting body of a doorless car, but with a grinding shriek the car tipped over, and bringing with it an avalanche of tangled metal, slipped a yard or two down the tip on which it had been perched, and threw the child out. The child got to its feet without a whimper, and stared round again. The Place itself might have been a pit, for all around it walls towered. On one side rose a featureless and windowless wall of a stained and leprous white, looming up to a fringe of broken glass, and on which the names of every sort of filth had been scrawled in deformed letters. Round two more sides hung the broken ends of terraces of houses, leaning on to huge structures of wooden props, and staring back at the child with the soot-lined blind sockets of fireplaces high above him. From behind the nearest terraces came a noise of demolition, repeated rumbling and an avalanching of brick, while a pinkish cloud of plaster-dust drifted across the backdrop of windowless rows waiting their turn. The child looked long in that direction.

Then it found a piece of plastic sheeting, half buried, and began painstakingly to scratch it out of the rubble. When it was freed, the child began to stretch it over the top of a hollow, weighing it down at the edges with handfuls of grime. But when the child tried to crawl beneath it, a gust of dirty wind with litter on its breath snatched at the plastic and tore it away.

The child sat down beside the roofless hollow, and looked at the Place again. On the fourth side lay a band of black water, and, rising sheer from this, a rumbling and hissing building. It was composed partly of brick, thickly crusted and scabbed with soot though the sore red beneath blistered through it here and there, and partly of soiled concrete. All over it a maze of corroded piping connected barrages of metal vats. Through unglazed arches a lurid light could be seen playing intermittently over the void within. Two huge chimneys rose to smear the sky above, and lower down the piping emitted gusts of stinking vapour. At the bottom, the walls excreted continuously into the black water, spewing arcs of hot smoking fluid with a stench that hurt the nostrils and brought tears to the eyes. As the child watched, a man passed across a narrow walkway through the vats. He seemed scarcely of human size, among the installations. He wore a silver boiler suit, a helmet and a face-mask, like someone kitted out for survival in the air of the wrong planet. He held an incomprehensible tool. He never looked down at the Place.

The child sat very still, staring, but nothing more moved in the Place except the vomiting liquid, and scavenging crows flapping their greasy black feathers over the rubbish dumps, gliding like smuts against the sky.

But soon the child himself was moving purposefully down towards the stretch of black water. There seemed down there to be a sort of hut thing, a box-like shelter, like the little kiosks roadmenders use. It had caught the child's eye.

There was indeed, at the water's edge, a battered steel sentry box, to which a few scraps of dark blue paint still clung. It was at one end of a tray-like object, massively built of riveted rusted iron, and decked at the other end with a few strakes of bare, weathered, splintered wood. The child stepped into the tray-like thing, and looked gloomily at the iron door of the sentry-box, stoutly barred and heavily padlocked. A rusty tin chimney projected from the roof of the box, suggesting all sorts of safety within. The child reached out, and wrenched at the padlock. Flakes of rust caked its wet palm. The child rubbed its hand on its rags, and tried again. The padlock tore through the rust-riddled plate into which it had been slotted, and came away in the child's hand.

Eagerly the child lifted the bar bolt, heaved the door open on squealing hinges, and went in. The darkness was dry. At once the child felt how wet it had become, and shivered, frowning into the gloom. A black stove stood beneath the chimney, with its dead fire spilled out across the floor. Opposite the stove was a bare wooden bench. The child sat down on it. It was cold. The child pulled the iron door shut. Now it was cold and dark. Sighing with relief the child stretched out on the bench, pillowing its head on its arms. There was a curious lack of solidity in the sentry box, as though it shifted slightly from time to time, or as though the child felt tiny spasms of dizzyness from cold. But soon the child slept.

When, some hours later, it pushed open the iron door again, the rain had stopped. A watery sun had risen high over the houses beside the Place, and was casting a blurred shadow of their roofs over the rubbish heaps, and playing con-tricks, diamonding every bit of can or broken glass. Even the black water was graced by a sullen gleam, and a slick or two of dirty rainbow. The child, however, was interested more in another change. It was no longer alone.

Another blue hut had appeared a little way along the water side, with smoke floating upwards from its chimney. A step away from it a workman was heaving something up a slope, and dumping it. The child scrambled out into the air, and tottered across the Place on his matchstick legs. He crouched on his haunches, and silently watched the workman.

The workman was sorting lengths of chain. They had been shackled together, and he was working with pliers, removing the pins from the shackles, and laying out the chain on the platform in front of his hut, in zigzag piles. He was wearing thick scruffy trousers held up with a leather belt that had itself lost its buckle and was tied with string. His blue shirt had frayed, leaving the white weft threads hanging in patches of fringe. He was tanned very brown. When the child had been staring for some time, the workman, without looking up, said, "Mornin." The child started violently, flinched almost, at being spoken to. Then, after a pause it said, "Can I ask yer somthink?"

"You can ask. T'aint to say you'll get told."

"How did I get here?"

"Ah," said the workman. He appeared deeply absorbed in the shackle he was opening. Then he looked up. His eyes were bright grey, oddly pale in his swarthy face.

"Best not reckon much o' that," he said.

"Oh," said the child.

"Here for long, then, are you?" said the man.

"Can't *stay* here," said the child. "Where could I go?"

"Well, see here ... er ... what's your name, then?"

"Don't know."

"You must know," said the man. "What does your mother call you?"

"She calls me that bugger, or that creep."

"I'd fix on Creep, out of those two," said the man. "I'm Jack. Pleased to meet yer."

"You haven't answered what I asked."

The man looked at the child again, with strange cloudy, rainlit eyes. "You asked me how you got here, and I said best not reckon. And you said you weren't stopping. Can't recall you asking owt else."

"Where could I go?" asked the child.

"Either way. Cut goes two ways from here, like from most places."

"Cut?"

"The canal." Jack gestured vaguely towards the stretch of black water. Then he plodded off, his heavy boots crunching the assorted rubbish on the ground, to fetch another length of chain.

Creep returned to the iron shelter, and sat beside it, looking, mystified, at the water. Far below him he saw the silver technician, upside down, crossing the catwalk with the incomprehensible tool in his hand. He could also see that what he had taken to be a pool, merely a larger version of the flashes of foul liquid on the dump behind him, could possibly be a continuing length of water, curving round the Place, and going somewhere, so that what looked like the end of it, was merely a sharp bend, cutting off the view. It did not look enticing, disappearing between two black scabrous walls, and it was dry and comfortably dark in the hut. He thought about it, this way and that.

"Still here, Creep?" called Jack in a while. "I thought you wasn't stopping!"

"*How* do I go?" asked Creep.

"You don't know much, son," said Jack. "Look here, then, and I'll show you." He bent, and lifted from among the weeds fringing the canal bank a length of chain fixed to the iron tray on which Creep's hut was built. He tugged hard, and up came a pin attached to the chain, bringing a clod of cindery earth up with it. When Jack tugged again the ground beneath Creep's feet began to glide forwards, gently and silently. The iron tray was a boat, floating free once the weeds that had grown into it from the bank were torn loose. Hut and all, it came along behind Jack as he pulled it. A step or two more, and he gave the end of the chain to Creep.

"All yours," he said.

Creep jumped to the bank and began to pull the chain. Slowly the flat and its cabin were drawn along, round the curve of the canal bank. A cindery overgrown path skirted the water, along which Creep could struggle, almost bent double, with the chain across his shoulder, and his thin legs splayed as he pulled. The rags on his emaciated body fluttered in the wind. The Place was left behind.

In a little way path and canal both passed under an elegant narrow cast-iron bridge, and joined a wider band of water, stretching away right and left. In both directions the banks of this wider canal were lined with dirty walls, and towered over by chimneys.

"Which way, mate?" called Jack from behind him. "I'll give you a hand turning it." The two of them stood for a moment looking left and right along the prospects of gloomy water.

"The cut goes on, or back, from here," said Jack.

"I'll go back," said Creep.

"Just as you say, gaffer," said Jack, taking and heaving the chain to turn the front of the boat.

Then the child leaned a bony shoulder into the iron links, and hauled again.

The canal continued for some distance between high soot-etched buildings on either side. Reflected walls hung black curtains into the water, and a narrow ribbon of sky lay between, far below. Where chimneys towered, a long tremulous ribbon of darkness dangled deep into the mirror world, that broke into bars, and dissolved as Creep pulled his boat over it. By and by, an unruly margin of dandelion and grass edged the water, a green ribbon threaded through the desert of brick and stone. Now and then a branch led off the canal into a foetid basin of dark water, clotted with a scum of floating rubbish. Iron bridges across the mouths of these branches rode in graceful low arches, and carried the towpath over and on. Creep would struggle, bent almost double by the labour of lifting the heavy chain up over the balustrade of the bridges. But once on the level again, he walked easily. The boat floated along smoothly and lightly behind him, seeming to go more and more easily; not as if he were pulling it exactly, but as if it were a dog on a lead at his side.

And then he came to a place where a black wooden gate closed off the canal. The towpath ascended a short flight of brick steps beside the gate; across the path, too, the gate set an obstacle—a heavy horizontal beam, painted black and white. Creep stopped.

His boat moved on, glided past him, overtook him. Too late he realised that it would stop only if he pulled it back, hard. He couldn't prevent it from banging into the gate, which juddered at the impact, and then swung open. It led into a slimy, narrow chamber, with another gate the other end. Creep looked at it, puzzled, standing with the chain in his hand.

A child appeared out of a cottage alongside, a little girl in a dirty pinafore. She was swinging a bent iron crank.

"Ast nivver seen a lock afore, then?" she demanded, looking scornfully at Creep.

"No," said Creep.

"Gawd," said the girl. "Well, tha'rt in luck. I'll do this one for ye, more or less. Get it in there, then!"

Creep climbed the steps, and stood on the edge of the narrow deep stone chamber, hauled on his clanking chain, and dragged the flat into the lock. Once he got it moving it was hard to stop, and banged loudly into the stone sill below the gate at the other end of the lock.

"Watch it! You'll wake me bloody father, and get a leathering!" said the girl, calmly.

Creep watched her lean on the beam, and close the gate. He watched her use her windlass to wind up the notched iron bar that opened the culvert, and let water into the lock. He watched the water boil and roll upwards till it filled the lock, and brought his boat up level with the ground he stood on. He helped her swing the top gate open, walking backwards with his buttocks thrust against the balance beam.

"Thanks," said Creep, and once more took up his chain.

Beyond the lock the buildings moved in closer to the canal. The ribbon of sky that wound along below, narrowed to the merest thread of light; Creep moved slowly, reluctant to go on. At last the dirty brick cliffs met; they closed right across the water, which disappeared beneath them into a black tunnel under an arch. Creep would never have gone in there had not his boat once more refused to stop. It glided on for yards under its own momentum after his feet had faltered and halted on the path. The archway was so black because another wooden lock-gate was shut across it, just a few yards in. The path narrowed, and climbed a flight of steps right in the bowels of the building. Creep stopped and looked, and thought for some time. This time the lock was full of water, and his boat was below. He climbed onto his boat, and went into the cabin. There he found what he had seen before without understanding it—a windlass rusted to a flaking orange colour, hanging on a hook. He used it to wind up the rack and pinion gear nearest himself; the water flowed away out of the lock, making his boat rock about and tug at its chain. When the water levelled and lay still, he opened the gates and hauled his boat in.

In a while he emerged, out from under the building, out of the lock, on to a tranquil stretch of water winding in a long curve past a church on a sloping green; past a row of houses with little gardens; past a pair of long black boats loaded with coal, and two horses grazing by the towpath, still tethered to the boats by long ropes. Behind them was a cottage, with a workshop beside it, topped by a huge chimney, belching smoke. Through the open door Creep could see fire, and hear voices, and a sound of hammering. "Whoa! Still, my beauty!" called a man's voice. Leaning up against the smithy door stood a man wearing boots to the knee, and a velvet jacket. He stared at Creep vacantly, as though he could see through and beyond him to something a way off; then he turned his head, and called, "Blacksmith! How much longer?" Creep passed by.

Sitting on a rusty anvil among the blacksmith's cabbages, in a garden plot beyond the forge, was a sooty boy about the same size as Creep. He wore a shirt with the sleeves torn off at the elbows, and his forearms were covered with blisters and red marks. He stared at Creep.

"Swap yer that chain for a nice bit of rope," he said. "Won't be half so heavy to draw along."

"All right," said Creep. There was a greedy glint in the boy's eye. But the rope he brought seemed good and thick, and was, as he said, much lighter and less bruising on Creep's shoulder as he leaned and tugged. One jerk on the rope, and the boat obligingly swam forwards. Creep looked back, meaning to wave or call, and saw the boy, answering a shout from the forge, jump up from his seat, leap on to a treadle by the forge chimney, and begin to jump up and down to work the bellows. Gusts of thick smoke puffed from the chimney in time with the boy's bobbing up and down.

Creep trudged on. And round the next corner he was in a new world. On one side the canal bank was formed of little cliffs of pink stone, and above them were woods, deep with green shadows, and wild flowers growing to the brink. On the other side of the canal he looked down from the towpath across a green valley with a little silver stream winding in it between meadows thick with buttercups and scattered with grazing cows; beyond, a low range of wooded hills closed the prospect. The shining highway of water curved away before him, following the swelling line of the hillside. And as he looked, he saw on a branch quite near him a little bird with a rusty breast, which flew in the same moment that he saw it, turning to a brilliant blue spark that burned along the surface of the canal, and disappeared into a distant tree. Creep stood still, and rubbed his eyes. His boat glided past him, and then nudged in beside the bank, coming to rest with a fringe of towpath weeds leaning over and into it, looking as if it hadn't moved for years. Creep looped its new rope to a tree, sat down on its rough deck, and stared. He stared for a long time, while the green light all around him faded to a soft grey, and the real and mirrored skies shifted from bright silver to soft lilac and pink.

At last he got up, meaning to put himself to bed on the cabin bench. "I never knew it was like this," he declared to an operatic thrush in the bush beside him. "And," he added in an aggrieved tone, "*he* never told me!"

2

Enclosed and cut off though it seemed, there must really have been ways into the Place from the surrounding streets, for a little while after Creep had departed, two more children appeared, weaving across the pits and mounds, calling to one another. These two, a boy and a girl, were unlike Creep. They were shabbily but decently clad. The boy had a carefully-darned sweater, the girl a quilted anorak against the cold. Their faces were rounded out and rosy, their legs and arms were straight and strong. They ran about, vigorously. There were obviously searching for something. The Place greeted them with little spurts of kicked-up dust, little avalanches of displaced dirt, reaching up to them, griming their socks, clinging to them, claiming them below the knees. After a while the girl began to cry.

"Hi!" called the boy, the need to call loudly distorting his voice to a manic scream. "Hi! To me! To me!"

He got no answer except the dismal croaking of crows, disturbed at their scavenging.

"He couldn't have got far over this," said the girl, sniffing, and rubbing tears away with the back of her hand, leaving a grimy watermark on her cheek. "Not without shoes, Chris. Look at it."

They both looked down at the sinister bright blades of broken glass pointed out by the thin sunlight. The girl shuddered. The boy looked morosely across the wastes and stared at the canal.

"There's water there," he said, swallowing hard.

"Oh, no!" cried the girl. They began to run. At the edge of the canal they stopped and stared at the greasy surface of the water. They saw the catwalk, drowned deep in the grimy depths, and a man passing upside down along it, not looking at the Place. They raised their eyes to the real man above them, and called, but he did not stop nor look.

"We've got to be *sure* he isn't here," said the boy. "We've looked everywhere else, Pauline. He might have hid away somewhere and got caught, he might of hid away in something and gone to sleep. We've got to look in all those old cars, and pipes, and drums and things, and behind everything."

"It'll take so long!" wailed the girl.

"What else could we do?" he said simply.

They divided, each taking an area of dump, and searched silently, for a long time. The girl got caught on a broken car-door, and tore a rent in her anorak. She was very small, not very good at looking; she kept going back to search the same places again. The boy was better, though he scratched his face and hands crawling over and under things. He was older—just beginning to grow long and gangling. The sleeves of his sweater did not reach to his wrists. It took them both a long time to make sure. But by and by they were standing again on the banks of the black water, looking at it with fear.

A noise behind them made them spin round. The workman had emerged from his boat hut, and was unfixing its mooring rope. The boat was full of sorted chain. He looked up as the children cannoned towards him, shouting.

"Have you seen—oh, have you seen a child here?" asked the boy.

"More'n one," said the workman. He returned the boy's anguished gaze with a cool, cloudy glance.

"Have you seen one here, on his own, today—a very little boy?"

"Looking for him, then, are you?"

"Oh, if we don't find him he'll die!" wailed the girl, tears flowing again.

"Making a real drama, you are," said the workman. "Kids get lost and found every day of the week. He's probably gone home to his mum while you're out looking for him."

"We don't think he would, you see," said the boy. "And we're very worried about him. He hadn't got a coat on; he must be very cold and hungry."

"He'll find his way, son," the workman said.

"He hadn't any shoes on. He couldn't swim."

"He'll have asked his way, and got himself back where he belongs."

"He din't *know* where!" cried the girl.

"We're, you see we're on a visit here," gabbled the boy, "and we think he didn't know the address."

"Not even the name of the road?"

"He couldn't read. He couldn't ask, hardly."

"A real littl'un, you mean. You'd best not muck about if he's really little. You'd best go to the police."

The two children cast terrified glances at each other, and the girl seized the boy, and clung to him.

"Not friends of yours?" said the workman. "But they're your best help to find a baby."

"He's not a baby," said the boy, and now there were tears in his eyes too. "Just very small, and well ... not very used to things."

"Ah. There was a kid here. Couldn't be your sort, though. Real scruff. Not looked after at all. Skin, bone and rag, only."

"Which way did he go?" asked the boy.

"Along the cut. Come with me a step, and I'll show you."

The man hauled his loaded flat a little way. He began to pull it along the towpath, with the two children following. They came to the main line of the canal, and glanced anxiously both ways, seeing nobody.

"Which way did he go?" asked the boy. "Left or right?"

"Left," said the workman. "And my way's right. Tara then. If you don't find him at first, keep after him."

The children hardly stopped to hear him, but made off down the towpath at a run, and had disappeared before Jack had drawn his flat round the corner, and begun to move it along his way.

They soon slowed down to a breathless trot. They pursued the towpath along, over the little iron bridges, past the factories, past the side-basins. In a while they came to a lock. Beside it stood a roofless cottage with windows boarded up. They scrambled into its garden and ran round it to see if there was a way in to hide in it, but it all seemed secure. The boy glanced for a moment at the unfenced fall into the slime-lined lock chamber, the dark water lying in wait at the foot of the walls. A cushion was floating in it, with its stuffing trailing out. The boy shuddered, and then ran on.

Some way beyond the lock the canal was all bridged over by dark buildings of scabby brick. At first they thought there was no way through, no way further; then they saw that the path went on, beside a subterranean lock, tunnelling through beneath the building, and they, too, went on, coming out the other side to see a wide green, and a church, and so to a long reach lined with wire fences, where various factories lined the canal bank, and notices announced that savage dogs patrolled the spaces beyond. Vast white buildings like cardboard boxes extended windowless behind the fences. Gleaming metal chimneys with spiral flanges on them rose above corrugated roofs. A huge gasholder, all lacy pale blue columns, its once blue walls triangulated with a geometry of rust stood opposite. A railway crossed overhead on an iron bridge. And just beyond the bridge there was a neat white cottage with clean curtains at its window and a little paling fence around it. A bicycle leant against the fence. The people who lived here, the boy saw, would need a bicycle—for there was no way to approach the cottage except along the towpath. Around the cottage, penned in by factory walls, was a kitchen garden, and projecting into the garden, against the side of the cottage, was a long low shed with two double doors. It was only one storey high, and finished in a massive tall brick chimney. A funny object, like a witch's hat as high as a child, and made all of iron, stood at the cottage porch.

"Look, Chris, he could be in those sheds," said the girl.

"We'd be trespassing," said the boy. "We'll have to

ask." They opened the little gate, and knocked at the horseshoe knocker on the door.

A woman with a flowery apron and grey hair opened it.

"We've lost our brother," said the girl. "He's only little, and he likes to hide. Has he been here?"

"I haven't seen a body all day, my duck," the woman said. "But if it puts your mind at rest, you have a good look round."

They thanked her. They looked. The doors of the shed were firmly closed and locked. There were some funny slots beside the chimney, but not even Pauline thought a child could have crawled in through those. As they scrambled round they saw a great pile of rusting iron stacked against the back wall of the shed— bars and rods of various sizes, and a huge heap of chain. But of the child they were looking for there was no sign.

Disconsolate now, walking slowly, kicking the towpath dust, they went on a few yards.

"He's drowned, that's what," said the girl, in a tight, dry little voice.

"Oh, don't, Pauley," said the boy. "He might not be. We'll just find him asleep somewhere. He sleeps at funny times, what with his day and night being much the same."

"He couldn't have got this far. You know he couldn't. He hadn't any shoes, and he couldn't move, hardly."

"I was doing exercises with him."

"*My* legs ache now, Chris, never mind what his would. I'm going off home."

"I'm not," said the boy. "Look, Pauline, you go, and you can tell Mum where I am. And if she won't do anything to help, you'll have to do what the man said, and get the p'lice."

"Oh no!" wailed Pauline. "I'm not going to tell her you're off on your own by the canal—she'll be worried out of her mind, and when she's worried she's cross. Come on home, Chris, do!"

"Not till I find him."

"Look," said Pauline, her voice all soft and wheedling. "Come home. He's drowned. And think, Chris, won't it be good really? You won't have to worry any more; you won't have to feel so bad about things. Everything will be just ordinary."

The boy turned away from her, and shook his head.

"We *are* just ordinary, 'cept for him," she said. And then when he made no move, "We could eat all our chips ourselves …"

"Go home, Pauley," he said, and went on down the overgrown path between a stretch of scruffy hedge and the grass and flower-fringed water.

Pauline watched him go. But when the towpath turned and he was out of sight she called after him, "Chris! *Christopher*!"

He did not call back, or return. She stood a moment; then, scuffing her toes in the towpath dust, she began to trail home.

3

There were voices in the morning. Voices close by the little flat boat, and something scraping lightly across the roof. The curled-up rags shifted suddenly as the child asleep within woke abruptly and completely. Shivering, Creep opened his heavy door, and looked out. There were men, and boats, and horses all around him. On the canal a line of black-hulled boats full of coal, weighed down deep in the water, was coming towards him. There were scraps of bright grimy paint on them, in fairground patterns. Along the bank trudged horses, towing. And along beside the horses ran little children, raggedly clad, leading the animals, and coaxing them on with sweet, high voices, calling obscenities. Away from Creep's staring gaze moved empty boats, riding high, with a stout woman at the tiller of the first, and stick-limbed girl at the tiller of the second. The tow-line of the empty boats rode at a high diagonal across the laden ones; the tow-line of the laden ones, dipped into the water, slipped beneath, rose snapping taut again, shaking off diamonds into the bright morning air, and crossed above Creep's head, scraping his boat cabin roof, repeating the sound that had woken him a minute since. A stout lad, warmly clad in a moleskin jacket, who was leading the horse along, frowned slightly as though he did not understand the movement of the rope, but he passed by without a word or a glance. Behind him came a tiny girl, leading a huge white horse. She had a bruised cheek, and a cut knee, and she bestowed on Creep a sudden toothless grin, and the words, "Mornin' yer poor bleeder!" as she went by.

On being spoken to, Creep said to nobody in particular, "Them's *horses*. And they're bigger'n what I'd of thought." He closed his eyes to remember the rag-book, with coloured pictures half worn off the cloth, which had supplied him with this information from the depths of memory. "But they don't bite," he told himself sagely.

The boats had passed on in either direction; the noise of the folk on them receded down the towpath. The water rocked back to smoothness and held a grey-green image of the world, splashed with green from bushes in young leaf, splashed with white where the blackthorn blossomed on its bare twigs. Creep looked at it with intense bafflement for long minutes. Then: "There's flowers what grow on trees," he said.

At last, there seeming little else to do, he unhitched his rope. Just then a pair of working boats overtook him. First the horse and his boy came by, then a length of rope passing over Creep's head, then a leading boat, laden low, with a man at the tiller, and then a butty boat, steered by a scrap of a girl wearing only petticoat and shawl, who called to him, "Want a tow? Tunnel's coming!" Her boat swung wide on the bend, nearly touching his, and as it passed she leant over, and dropped a loop of line over the cleat at the front end of Creep's boat. At once the little flat was drawn along behind hers, and Creep had to run and jump aboard it, and coil up the wet length of his own rope as they went along.

At first he could see only the wide wooden rudder of the girl's boat, with a fine white horsetail dangling from it, but in a while she reached a hand to him, and he jumped up and stood beside her. Three in line, they were moving in a deep cutting, lined with trees and roofed with sun-shot leaves. Primroses grew at the water's edge, and little specks of purple and white showed where wild violets shaded beneath the trees. Suddenly the way forward was closed by a rose-pink brick wall in which was a black archway. There was a pause; the towlines slackened. The boy ahead cast the towrope off the horse, and led the animal away up a narrow steep path over the top of the tunnel mouth. Then there were voices, bargaining up at the leading boat. Then very slowly they all began to move again.

"Scared of the dark?" said the girl.

"No. Used to it," said Creep. But he was not used to tunnels. The darkness was a long oval arch, above and below them. Strapped on to planks at the front of the boat, lay men suspended on their backs over the water, and walking with their legs against the walls. Their shadows strode vastly in the dim light of lanterns. The roof dripped. They passed under an air shaft, below which a column of faint dusk stood upon the water; behind them the daylight disc of the tunnel entrance dimmed to golden yellow, and then, still smaller, began to glow softly red. In a while the leggers in their terrible striding began to sing, and the tunnel took their voices, and loomed them along the darkness in a vibrant blurred booming. Creep clung to the cabin roof, standing beside the girl on the butty boat, with his eyes wide open, staring. He should have been in the way of the swing of the long tiller arm, but he seemed not to be. And little by little the disc of light in front of them enlarged: it filled in with details, white, green; sky and leaf beyond reflected double, above and below the unseen water-line. The light filtered in towards them, creeping in a thin shine along the crooked lines of wet brickwork overhead; and then suddenly the full blaze of daylight struck them, and the world opened out wide on either side.

"We'm stopping here," the girl said, pointing to a wharf and a line of cottages just beyond the end of the tunnel. "Tara, then," and she unhitched Creep's rope, and dropped it lightly on the deck of his flat. He jumped aboard, and, carried on by its own momentum, his boat glided on, overtaking the other two, and leaving his friendly helper far behind. He was astonished at how far, and how smoothly the movement of his boat continued; but as it did continue and seemed not to slow down, he sat down on the splintery wooden deck, and watched the world go by, for yards and yards, and shortly miles and miles around him.

Beyond the tunnel the canal ran for a while along the side of a hill, so that Creep had a view, first of fields, and then of a town below him. The town had black chimneys rising thick as city church spires over its roofs, and it was made of soot-etched stone, and slate, and grey streets packed tight and narrowly together. Between houses Creep glimpsed cramped and tiny yards, and houses standing open to these yards only, facing not even so much as a length of muddy lane. Children ran about. Crowds of squat chimneys smoked on the roofs, and the dark bulk of factories rose over all.

Gliding above this town, for the canal crossed it on an embankment, Creep looked at it with distaste. It reminded him of the Place.

On the outskirts of the town stood a church that had once been a parish church in a village, no doubt, now so blackened by the smoky air that it might have been cut out of coal. Beyond the church Creep was in green fields again, though nothing grew there, only a few thin cows and a goat or two were tethered to graze, between dusty bushes. It was here that Creep began to notice that the silent water on which he floated along was changing. It had been clear, with green weeds growing deep and shiny below him; it had become a murky muddy colour long before the tunnel. Now it was turning rusty red. Red-brown, at first; then brilliant russet, like tinned tomato soup; then darkening and thickening to an angry sunset shade tending to the colour of blood. Creep was alarmed by it, would have liked to stop, but did not know how. The boat was well in mid-stream, too far from either bank for him to jump for it, and seemed now to be speeding up, sweeping him onwards.

And then the canal swung round a bend, and approached a steep cliff. There were wharves, coalyards, people shovelling and shouting. In the face of the rocky cliff two little low arches like tiny tunnels were cut, with a wharf between them. Creep's boat moved smoothly towards the right-hand of these entries, and though he cried out in alarm he could think of no way to stop it. As he was carried into the darkness he looked up, and caught just one glimpse of trees growing green above, and a church spire atop the cliff, against the sky. Then he was moving helplessly in pitch blackness.

Compared to the tunnel, this was as black as hell. So thick and close did the darkness feel, that it seemed to Creep he could feel it parting as he moved through it, and brushing against his face. And it smelt: a wet, gritty mineral smell with an acrid edge to it. He did not know how far he had come—it seemed a long way— before he saw light ahead of him; then the boat swept him through a golden pool of faint lamplight, and he saw, as he passed, an underground wharf, very narrow and low, and a group of figures labouring there, shovelling coal from wooden corves on sledge rails into thin narrow barges tied up on the black water. Some, it seemed, were men, and some women, their shirts open to the waist, their blackened breasts shining with sweat. Then he was past them, unseen, and moving even further into the depths of the earth.

Several times he passed little caverns hewn out of the grey shale, from which passages and tunnels departed mysteriously into the workings. And at one of these his boat came quietly and gently to a halt. The stub end of a tallow candle, fixed with a blob of wax to a foothold on the wall, showed Creep a web of narrow passages, barely high enough for a child to stand up in, cut from rock so black it seemed that darkness itself had solidified. And from somewhere in these horrible recesses Creep could hear crying. Someone was crying down there, in terrified wailing sobs, racking the body that emitted them, leaving long gasps for breath, and then beginning again. A high-pitched human voice; a child's.

Creep sat and listened. He was waiting for the adult to come and deal out blows and curses. But although some way off in another direction he could hear adult voices, and something rumbling, and the ring of pick or shovel blows on stone, nobody came, and the cries continued. At last, when the stub of candle guttered, and brightened on the verge of going out, Creep heaved a deep trembling sigh, and went to look for the crying himself.

He took the wrong tunnel at first. Scrambling, doubled up, along it he came to a heavy wooden door, and beside that a little hollow cut out of the tunnel wall, in which a tiny, dirty girl, with a head of grimy curls was asleep, her knees hugged to her chest, and her head drooped upon them, her candle end burning on a ledge above her. She woke up with a start as Creep came by, and pulling on a cord she opened a door across the tunnel in front of him, He passed, and heard it thump closed behind him. Beyond it the sound of work was louder. Soon Creep came to a place where men were lying on their sides, hewing coal from a narrow seam with pickaxes. The roof was so low that everybody was crawling. A boy with a shovel removed the coal that the pick had loosened, heaving it into a wooden sled, and, Creep saw, attached to the sled by a chain, going between her legs to a belt about her waist, was a girl on hands and knees, with a candle strapped to her forehead.

When the sled was full she began to crawl away, drawing it after her on the rough ground through an inch or two of thick and filthy water, seeping up from the ground, and a thin boy came, and put his head up against the back of the sled, and began to thrust at it to help the weight along.

Creep said, "Someone's crying. Someone's lost." And nobody looked up, or turned, or answered, except a half-naked girl not much bigger than he, chained to an empty sled, waiting her turn, who looked at him, and said, "Poor little trapper, 'ast tha lost thy road? I'll guide thee to thy trap," and to her voice a growl of rage from a huge man plying a pick replied, "Thee mind thee own job, and stay theer, else I'll belt thee!"

The girl said to Creep in a whisper, "Jack Wither's girl is lost since yestern', I heard tell. Happen it's her."

Creep retreated. He went back to the waterside, feeling his way in darkness till he heard the water plashing at his feet, then turning about, he followed the sound of sobbing down another passage, his hands held out before his face to feel the way by. He hit his head more than once on a low outcrop of roof. His feet were in water over his ankles, and his wading steps made splashing sounds. Grit from the walls stuck to his fingers as he trailed them over rock, finding his way. But the crying grew steadily louder. Once he seemed to have passed it, and heard it growing fainter behind him, but retracing his steps, he found a gap in the wall, which he had passed by the first time, and from which the voice sounded very clearly. One or two more steps, and suddenly his extended hand met something soft, damp, and the voice shrieked right in his ear. Something grabbed hold of his neck very tightly, and cried, " 'Elp me out, 'elp me out!"

Creep clutched the tiny wrists and dragged them down. "Leggo!" he shouted.

He felt the frantic little bony fingers laced in his ragged clothes. "S'all right," he said. " 'Aven't I come for yer? I'm not going to run off and leave yer."

A small sob answered him.

" 'Aven't yer got a candle?" he enquired.

"I've etten it," the voice replied.

"Yer *what*?"

"The rats've run off wi' me bait, and I'm near clemmed."

"You keep ahold of me then. Right?"

"I can't walk hardly. I walked so far in the dark I'm all fagged out," said the voice, sobbing again.

"Not far," lied Creep, encouragingly.

But as he dragged her back, groping towards what he hoped was the gap in the wall where he had turned off from a better road, he could suddenly see. There were lights in the roadway. Here came three men, stooping to go along, and carrying lanterns, who whooped and called, and hastened towards Creep. By their lights he saw that the voice and the clinging hands belonged to a tiny girl with yellow hair, barefoot and in rags, who ran towards the searchers, arms held out.

"There, lass, us'll tek thee to thee Dad," said one of them.

"Him too?" she said.

"Him?"

"There was a boy found me, and brought me this far," she said.

"What sort of boy, then?" another asked her, looking straight at Creep.

"He were little, and kind."

"God help us, another trapper wandering loose! Dost thee know where he's to, lass?"

"He was here, just now."

"She's dreaming, mostlike."

"No wonder, being so long i' the dark. Coom, now, wench." And one of them took her up in his arms, and turned away, and another went close behind him. But the third stared at the wall behind Creep, and frowned. He had pale grey eyes, like the sky on a cloudy day. "If

34

th'art a trapper, go back to thee door, and keep it," he said, softly. "If the door isn't kept the air don't flow; and if the air don't flow where it ought there's choke damp that fells usn where we work, or firedamp—but one spark and yon blows us all to hell. So keep thy door, and stay by it."

Creep shrank away from him, startled at being spoken to by an adult, and raised his hands as though afraid of blows.

"But if, as I do think, thou art no trapper, but a Knocker, or suchlike sprite, we do thank thee for finding Sarey, and beg thee to go back where thou cumst from."

"What keeps thee, Jack?" called one of the others back to him.

Jack turned to follow away. Creep sat against the wall, and watched the lights recede. A huge black outline of Jack filled the little passageway as he bore his lamp away before him.

But before they had gone out of sight down the long tunnel, there came from somewhere beyond them a horrible scream, followed by another and another, and a crashing sound, and a roar of rage, and a voice swearing.

"Bloody hell, what's about now?" said one of the men.

"Greenwood lamming into his prentice, again, I'll be bound," said Jack. They all ran forward, and Creep, like a moth drawn to the vanishing light, scrambled after them. They came to a stall cut out of coal, in which a huge man, near naked, gleaming with sweat, and black as the coal he laboured in, stood and bellowed at a stocky little boy. They all saw the man pick up the child and hurl him bodily against the wall of coal. The boy lay stunned, and the man bellowed at him to get up and carry, and when he still lay, staring stupidly, kicked at him, and swung his pick.

The pick was seized in mid-swing by Jack, who said, "For the love of Christ, Bill, dost thee want the magistrate down on thee again?"

"Sod the magistrate!" cried Bill. "How can I fare if the bleeder won't carry my coal?"

"He's forweary. And it's nearly loose time. Give over."

"And lose the last corve?" yelled the other. By this time the boy had staggered to his feet again, and the man bent, and with muscles bowed at the strain lifted a huge lump of coal, and laid it in a sling on the child's back. The boy fell at once to his knees.

"Give over now," said the man on Jack's right, with a very meaning edge to his voice. "Leave 'un be, else I'll speak to the overlooker myself. Come off with us now, d'ye hear?" and he took the miner's one arm, while Jack took the other, and dragged him away between them, while the third man came behind, carrying the little girl fast asleep in his arms. The boy lay pressed to the ground by the load of coal on his back, groaning, and with his eyes shut. Creep crouched down beside him, and watched, silent, while the lantern-light falling behind the departing men dimmed and vanished away. Then in the dark he reached out a hand, and whispered, "Are you dead?"

"Might as well be," said the boy. Creep rolled the coal off his back, and waited. "Ah, I'll not endure it!" the boy said. "I'll run away, so I will! Only he'd belt me so were I found and brought back to him...."

"I know a way out," Creep remarked.

"He were given a sovereign by the poorhouse

master to buy me clothes when I was bound his prentice ..." the boy said, muttering to himself, in a voice that swayed past Creep as though he were rocking himself to and fro. "... ah never spent it. It's rags I go in, and not even clogs to me feet...."

"Come on, then," said Creep.

"T'isn't the work I mind; I baint any shirker," the boy moaned on. "But that man half murthers me when he's doing badly. Twice I've had his pick in my bottom. Last time hasn't mended, and he'd a done it again if the others hadn't happened by.... Ey, harken!"

"I can't hear nothing," said Creep.

"That's just it, fule! The men have all broken shift, and gone off; us'll be trapped here all night if us baint at the shaft directly!"

"I know another way out," said Creep. "Come with me." And he took a firm hold of a rag or two on the boy, and pulled.

"Can't see thee," said the boy. "Who art 'ee?"

"Creep. Who are you?"

"I'm Tom Moorhouse, Bill Greenwood's butty. Where are tha teking me?"

"Out of here," said Creep.

Like a creature born in darkness, Creep moved along the tunnels. He retraced his steps without faltering, and came at last to a place where the splash of drips from the roof told him there was water. He groped about, and found his boat. They both got into it; it rocked and then settled.

"Tom," said Creep, "how do they move these boats along, down here?"

"Ah," said Tom, "we're going the road the coal goes, is it? There's iron staples in the roof, and on the walls. They grabs on those, and pulls the boats along."

Creep stood up, and groped at the darkness. Soon he found a staple and heaved on it. The boat slipped a little. Tom stood up to help him, groaning as he moved. But when they had found and pulled on some dozen of the invisible handholds the boat seemed suddenly lighter, easier to shift, until it was carrying them past the staples before they had time to pull on them. It had begun to go of its own accord again, and it seemed to be moving very fast. They sat down, out of harm's way. They heard the water gurgling under the blunt prow of the flat. Then suddenly the damp close air was swept through with coolness and a sense of space. There was no light, but there was a breath of wind on their faces, smelling of warm leaves, of waterweed. Looking up, Creep saw a scatter of bright stars. They had come into the open again, but it was night. A moon swam up from behind a rag of cloud, and Creep saw that Tom, beside him, was stretched out on the bare deck, fast asleep, and the boat itself was moving steadily onwards over the quiet water of the cut.

4

Christopher kept walking. The towpath moved out into open country. There were pink stone cliffs, and woodlands. There were fields and cows. The path became harder and harder to follow. It was deep in grasses and flowers, dog-daisy and dandelion. The thorn bushes of the hedgerow beside it reached prickly arms across his way, growing uncut for seasons. There were many places where the path had simply collapsed into the water, leaving a muddy steep slippery gap, round which the footholds were precarious. He struggled round somehow, getting a plimsoll full of water more than once, getting muddy and scratched and stung by nettles, but doggedly persisting.

The harder the going got, the more miserable he became. At last he sat down abruptly on a pile of wooden planks stacked up by a bridge, and said aloud, "He can't have got this far. Can't have."

The warmth of the sun was just softening a little, fading to an evening gentleness, and as soon as he sat down he felt bone weary. "And what's the use," he asked himself, "of looking *here* for someone much less strong, much less healthy than me?" He sighed. "If I'm tired," he told the bridge, "he'd be just dead beat.

He couldn't have got this far. I've passed him somehow."

291 said the bridge on a cast-iron plaque. It was a fine bridge, rose-red edged with black, and curving handsomely to the waterline. It seemed to have been made only for cows, for no road, nor even a path ran over it.

"It's just that I *haven't* passed him," Christopher said. "I know I haven't, somehow. Something terrible has happened, and I can't think what. He could have drowned, of course ... but I feel as if he hadn't. ... I feel as if he was somewhere.... 'Keep after him,' that man said. ..." But his legs were aching, now. He was hot. He was thirsty. Soon he stretched out along the top plank of the pile, meaning only to rest for a moment, and in a moment was fast asleep.

When he woke, it was dusk. Through the bridge ahead of him lay a long reach of glassy-still water. A dusty silver green clouded the surface. The reflections that had shone so clearly in daylight were obscured now by the low-angled evening light, by the fine powdering of floating seed and willow-down which lay on the water. There was nothing in sight along the canal bank except trees and fields. And back the way he had come tall trees leaned over the water. It was nearly dark—too dark, obviously, to make his way safely back across the holes and snags, and through the nettle and thorn patches that had beset his way even in full daylight. He wondered if he could get through the hedge and walk home in the fields. He scrambled up beside the bridge. Rabbits, startled in the empty meadow, scampered away, flashing white tails at him. The details of the land even a field away were obscured by the tender veils of dusk. He would get lost.

For a moment he was frantic; he ran back and forth across the bridge; he beat his clenched fists on the black brick parapet.

Then he thought that it was so late that someone would surely come and look for him. "Pauline will've told Mum," he told himself. "She'll send someone. She'll get the Welfare, or the p'lice to look for me." And with the thought came a spasm of pain for the other, for whom they would not be looking. He found himself facing the thought he had been avoiding all day. Perhaps *he* wasn't lost ... perhaps he was hiding ... not wanting to be found ... perhaps he was escaping. After all, what was there for *him* to come back to? Christopher thought of the black triangular door of the cupboard under the stairs opening, and the stale dirty smell that wafted from it, and of his own warm bed, with three shabby red blankets, and of the supper plate of bread and marge, the bag of crisps and the bottle of Tizer waiting for him at home. Longing for them, Christopher began to cry, wanting them, hating them, feeling horrible, feeling sick and cruel, hating his own food, his own bed. "If they're looking for just me," he said, "I hope they don't find me! I don't want to be found!" Miserably he remembered once, long ago, when their mother still sometimes let people into the house, sometimes gave them cups of tea at the kitchen table, somebody seeing Creep, and saying, "It's terrible! It's like the bad old days!" They had moved house twice since then. It had got worse and worse.

"Even his name isn't a real one," said Christopher. "Just swearing. What has he got to come back for?" And then, in a voice thick with tears, he said, "There was me. There *was* me. I tried my best! Oh, Creep, *I*

41

liked you! I did, I did! Oh, Creep, where are you? Oh, Creep, come back!"

And out of the silence, as if in reply, came a sudden volley of sounds, the ring of metal striking metal from just beyond the bridge. Christopher ran through the bridge arch, and stared. A man with grey hair and a brown moustache, in a worn corduroy jacket was wielding a heavy hammer, driving an iron spike into the path. Round the spike was a rope, and at the other end of the rope was a boat, snug alongside the weedy fringe of the path. Golden, butter-yellow light fell from its windows and threw melted pools of yellow into the dark water. A smell of bacon frying wafted through the open cabin door.

"Hullo!" said the man pleasantly, looking up from fastening his rope. "Where did you spring from?" Then as he caught sight of the boy's tear-smirched face he called out, "Jenny! Put some more bacon in that pan!"

5

Creep watched the stars for a while, then he curled up on the bench in his cabin, behind the iron door, and slept, leaving Tom stretched out in the open, on the deck. He didn't like to close the door on his companion, and so slept shivering on the draught of cool night air.

Sometime in the deep of the night, the boat stopped, gently coming to rest against the bank. Perhaps that alone would not have been enough to wake Creep, but the place where the boat had come to rest was brilliantly lit. Fiery light poured in upon his face, and when he opened his eyes the edges of the boat and of Tom's ragged sleeping form were drawn in bright outline as by a pencil of fire.

Creep got up, and looked out.

They seemed to have come to the mouth of hell. The sky blazed red and orange like the fiercest sunset possible; the torn masses of clouds were all glowing, and banners of red and black smoke rose across them. Somewhere to the right a pale moon cast a small pool of silver. There was a stretch of still water of some kind

below them, for the sky was redoubled in brilliant
reflection. And at the heart, at the centre of this fearful
combustion, the light glared gold instead of red, and
within the gold it blazed white, so that it seared the eyes
and closed the lids of the dazzled onlooker. Creep
turned away, covering his eyes. But the moment he
was not looking, he became aware of the noises. A
huge sighing swept across the valley, a sound like the
breaking of a vast wave on an immense shore. Then,
after a pause of only a moment, came another such. It
was as though some monster filled the valley, gasping
for breath. Far and faint across this terrifying sound
there floated up to Creep a cry or two—men shouting
somewhere below.

Creep trembled from head to foot. "Not here,
boat!" he said. He tried to shift the boat, jumping to
the bank, taking the rope over his shoulder, and
pulling, pulling, hoping to start it moving again, but it
seemed stuck fast. Red grass grew round his bare feet
as he pulled; a soft breeze stirred red leaves on dimly
visible trees. Firelight shone on the whole world, earth
and sky. Through spread fingers Creep looked once
again towards the source of the light. It was indeed a
horrible and vast fire, blazing white. Around it were
red molten mountains, and a few cottages, buildings,
and squat square chimneys, made all of bricks of fire.
The monstrous breathing came from down there
somewhere. There wafted up to Creep a gust of warm
air, smelling of hot dirt, of fire-irons. Then he heard a
roaring noise like a million stones tumbled all together
down a slope. The blaze dimmed down for a long
moment, and beyond it Creep saw a long row of
buildings full of the white fire, so bright that the
shadows of the pillars holding up the roof cast huge

stripes on the tall sky, like the black spokes of a wheel.

Whimpering a little to himself, and still unable to budge the boat an inch, Creep stepped over the unmoving body of Tom, who lay in a sleep like death, crept back into the cabin, and lay down, turning his face to the wall, and wrapping his jacket round his head to shut out sight.

Tom woke him. Tom shook him, then lifted him bodily off the shelf in the cabin, and set him down standing on the floor.

"Tha'rt real, then," Tom said. "Thowt a' must ha' dreamed thee. Th'art peaky enough to have bin dreamed up. Where ast tha brought us to?"

"Don't know," said Creep.

"How far have us come? They'll have the constables out looking for me, soon as they see I've skipped the shift. Got caught last time, and took back." His face puckered up for a moment as though he would cry.

"We come a long way, I think," said Creep. "We was moving fast, long after you was asleep."

"Happen we're all right, then. Come on!"

"Where?"

"Down the valley. Find summat to eat, afore all else."

"I'm not going down there!" cried Creep. And putting his head round the door, he gazed in the direction in which the fires of hell had blazed the night before.

It was a clear, bright, sunny morning. And they were looking from above into a steep-sided, winding wooded valley, descending towards a brown rapid river, beyond which the prospect was closed by another wooded hill. All was fair and green, and birds were singing in the leafy glades. The pool that had burned molten red last night lay serenely now, reflecting a clear blue sky, paler than the sheets of bluebells that lay like mirage water below the trees. But down the middle of this valley was a long smirch of black. There were chimneys, from which thick smoke bellied and poured upwards into the sky, and a cluster of black buildings, from among which, outshone and shrunken by the cool bright daylight, the white glow could still be seen. The trees down there were shrivelled; what leaves they had left were darkened with smuts and grime. And the sound of the great beast breathing still reached Creep's ears, though across it was a jumble of other noises—metal clanging, rumbles, voices, clatter.

"I'm not going down there!" Creep said again.

"It's a foundry," said Tom. "A big un. Nothing to be feared of, Creep. There'll be folk, and we'll beg a bite to eat." He shook his head. "Now I come to think ont, isn't a foundry for miles, and many miles. It's a tricksy thing to have come away so far. That bugger Bill Greenwood must wear his clogs thin if he'll come after me!" And he grinned broadly. "Come on!"

Creep followed timidly, a pace or two behind Tom who scampered at first, then went more carefully as the way grew steeper. They found a path to follow through the wood, that went down along a little precipitate stream fast falling down the valley. Tom stopped at a pool where a boulder stemmed the stream, and washed his face, and hands and arms, rubbing the coal dust off his body with the icy water, and handfuls of grass. "Mustn't be known for a collier," he told Creep. "Us can be sent back anytime." He managed, not to get clean, but to reduce the dirt on his body to a general grime of undistinguishable origin, a grey smear, instead of the black dust of the mine. Then they went down further.

The large pool they had seen from the canal was made by a wide and well-made dam across the valley. Out of it the water flowed very fast, scouring a narrow race that hugged the valley side, and disappeared round a turn of the hillside. The noise and din were loud and near, and smoke hung about them now, like a mist in winter, seeping the warmth out of the sun, spreading a bonfire mirk in the air. The fresh new leaves unfurled clean from black sooty twigs, black crusted trunks, bearing the burden of last year's smoke, and the year before's. But there was a neat row of cottages along the path beyond the pool, with little patches of garden in front of them.

At the open door of the first cottage was a young woman in a clean white apron, casting food to the hens.

"Spare us a bite, Missus?" Tom said to her. She looked at him long and calmly, with mild unworried eyes. Then she turned within for a moment, and brought him a bowl of gruel, with a drop of treacle as a savour, and a wooden spoon, which she gave into his hand. Tom's whole body stiffened at the sight and smell of it. He went down on his haunches at the garden gate, and shovelled spoonfuls into his mouth, hardly leaving time to swallow one before thrusting in another. Then he slowed up, and licked the last mouthful off the spoon repeatedly, long after it had been cleaned of the slightest trace. He rubbed his fingers round the bowl, and licked them clean. He sighed, and a cat-like dreamy expression drifted over his pinched features. All the while the woman watched him from the door.

At last he took back the bowl and spoon, and said, "Could you spare some for me mate, here?" and he gestured vaguely towards Creep. The woman frowned, but she put a ladle into her pot, and filled the bowl again.

Tom offered the bowl to Creep. Somehow it didn't attract him. "I'm not hungry, Tom," he said. "You have it." Tom still held the bowl out, but his hand wavered.

"Honest I'm not," said Creep.

"Th'art an odd 'un," said Tom, looking troubled. "It's *for* thee." But when Creep still reached out no hand to take it, Tom suddenly dipped the spoon, and ate the second bowl as avidly as he had the first.

"Thou hadst no need to lie, friend, to have what thou needest from me," said the woman sadly, from behind him.

"He..." began Tom, and then his voice trailed away, and he cast an odd, almost frightened glance at Creep. But Creep, looking on with his brown eyes brightly darting, seemed to notice nothing strange.

"Now if thy hunger is staunched, friend, best tell me where thou art from," the woman said.

Tom looked silently at her for a space. "I have come a good way," he said. "And I am going about to find work."

"Adam!" the woman called, and at once a man came from within, and frowned down at Tom. "Where thinkest thou a lad might find work?"

The man was wearing a leather apron, and his huge muscular arms were covered with pits and scars. He looked hard at Tom.

"Not for a runaway," he said, shaking his head. "Thou art too soft, Sarah."

"Wilt not so much as ask him what he runs from?" she said, her voice still level and quiet.

"Well, well. What camest thou from, boy?" said the man.

For answer Tom scuttled in through the door, and stood by the hearth, behind a chair, and let his ragged breeches fall, and lifted his tattered shirt. Creep sliding up to the threshold saw the marks on Tom's body. No change of expression crossed his face, but the cottagers, man and woman, exchanged glances, urgently, over Tom's head.

"I will have nought to do with sending him back to his master, Adam," the woman said, firmly.

"He's a strong enough lad," said Adam. "Perhaps he can work at chain and nails."

She pulled a face, and he went on impatiently, "Better than nothing, Sarah; better than starve, and better than *that*," with a tilt of his head towards Tom, who was quietly fixing his belt. "Come with me, and I'll show thee the way as I go down to work," he said, deciding.

Tom followed him out. His road went past the pool, "the Furnace Pool" he called it, along the race to the very heart of the smoke, the source of the fire, the source of the panting breathing that filled the valley.

"What dost thou think of that?" he said to Tom. And *that* was indeed something to think about. The captive water shot from the race, and poured from above over a huge water wheel; the wheel turned a shaft, and cogs on the shaft caught upon two huge bellows, and thrust them shut, blowing them alternately. They blew from left and right into an arch in a bastion of blackened brick, and, fanned to fury by their gusts, a fire raged within, and burned in a blazing jet from the top of the furnace. Here was the giant breathing, the hell's mouth glow! Along a platform to this mouth of fire men ran with barrows, tipping into the pit loads of ironstone, limestone and coke. At each load the blaze dimmed briefly, and then resumed its fury.

"Thou shouldst see the iron flow when we tap the furnace," said Adam, with pride. "We can make anything. Why, we are to make a bridge of all iron, to span the river o'er."

"Can I work here, master?" said Tom.

"Thou must grow a span first. 'Tis all man's work here. We work for the finest Ironmaster in England, the first to find how to make iron using coals, instead of charcoal."

"Is that good?" said Tom.

"Why, lad, we have needed more iron than we could grow trees for the smelting. And now the world shall be full of iron things, strong and cheap and handy, and the trees still growing green!"

He led them on, and below the furnace they came to another pool, where the water flowing away from the tail of the wheel that worked the bellows was gathered behind a second dam, and discharged over another wheel. This, Adam told Tom, was the Forge Pool. With clatter and splash the second wheel repeatedly lifted and let fall a massive iron hammer within the forge— the boys could see it within the workshop through the arched door—and beneath the hammer men were pulling iron bars, blazing hot from the hearth of a second furnace. Sparks and fragments of the red hot metal flew about, and each blow of the hammer exploded and hurt the ears, leaving a ghostly ringing behind it that tingled till the next blow struck. Looking away, Creep saw the bright ghost of the ingot beneath the hammer drifting across the green screen of hanging woods above him.

Below the Forge Pool yet another pool filled a leat to drive another wheel that turned rollers and cutters for making the iron into plates and rods. The two boys stared at that also. But there were no children working here, only sturdy men. "Here I'll take leave of thee," said Adam. "Go and ask along the rows down yonder, and I wish you may fare well."

So at last they came down to the bottom of the valley, where it widened out, and met the river. Here there were wharves and warehouses, and barges with masts and furled sails tied up for loading. Along the waterfront were the nailors' cottages to which Adam had directed them. Coming to the first one, Tom knocked upon the door.

There was no work for Tom there, nor anywhere along the row. But at the last cottage an old man told him that work for nailors was at the great town twenty mile off, mostly, and that if he was lucky he might beg a ride there on a load of iron rods.

"Will tha go back to the boat, then?" Tom asked Creep. They were riding back to back, perched on a huge mound of bright new rods, in a creaking cart drawn by a pair of mules. These poor beasts, under the carter's whip, were drawing their burden back up the valley towards the canal.

"Think I'll go with you," said Creep. "There's always been ... I'm used to a big boy to help me."

"I've done nowt for thee," said Tom. "Daft ha'p'orth!"

"You shared your porridge."

"You didn't eat none!"

But Tom said no more about Creep leaving, even when the cart crossed a little hump-backed bridge over the canal, and began to rumble and clang across a wooded plain.

They came in a while to a desolate rolling heath, covered with dirty grass, and stunted trees, from the face of which the fair spring day was masked by a wintery fog of smoke. Dotted around on this waste were little brick huts and sheds, each having a pile of coal lying at the door, and a chimney pouring soot into the sky, and a drift of smuts over the ground. From each of them came a din and clatter, the ring of metal upon metal. As the cart rumbled onwards, the brick dens and chimneys crowded in upon the road, until at last there was nothing but brick and smoke, and they had come into a town. A sullen, stormy, thundery light filtered through the smoke to show them the narrow gunnels of this place. Rutted and muddy like country tracks, fouled with piles of rubbish, a web of little passageways led through the rows of tiny blackened houses, and through alleys among a forest of chimneys. Almost every house had a smoking, clanging shed leaning up to it; and the air smelt hot and metallic.

The cart swung suddenly into a yard. There were sheds round it, full of iron rods. A man in a clean shirt sat at a table with a huge scale standing at his elbow. He was writing in a book. Before him stood a long line of folk, women and children, and one or two men, all in rags and blackened aprons. Tom and Creep scrambled off the cart, and rubbed their grooved and aching buttocks. They stood, watching.

One by one the waiting people took onto their shoulders a weighed load of rods, and, bending under the burden, walked away. There were folk coming as well as going; a woman came as they watched, hardly able to walk beneath a huge load of chain that bent her nearly double. The boys watched the load of chain being weighed and paid for, coins counted into an anxious hand. But instead of standing straight, the woman took a load of rods on her shoulders when she left. The iron rods and links jangled and rang; the master at the table spoke briefly to each rod bearer; from farther off, the racket of smithy work and hammering could be heard, but nearer, in the yard where they stood, it was oddly silent. The crowd of folk waiting seemed to have no urge to pass the time of day with one another. Their faces were haggard, and a curious colour, as though the dirt on their skin overlay not a flesh and blood hue, but the leached pallor of creatures that live in sunless places.

The carter, having unloaded his rods into the store, went and spoke with the master. Then he beckoned Tom. The master looked Tom over long and hard, and then nodded.

"Who wants a boy?" he asked. Nobody answered. "Nobody?" said the master.

"I'll tek 'un," said a voice from the back of the line.

"Thowt tha had a new boy not so long back," said the master.

"He broke his arm. I turned 'im off," the man said.

"Hear that, did you?" said the master to Tom. 'Mind and look sharp about you, and keep fit for work."

"Please, sir," said Tom, "what wages will I have with him?"

The master frowned. "I don't know that," he said. Then addressing no one in particular, "What wages do you give then, for dollying and blowing?"

"Nowt but his bait, while he learns; say a week or two. Three shilling a week, after."

Tom nodded. And then he and Creep followed their new master out of the yard. At the gate he stopped, picked up his load of iron rod, and laid it across Tom's shoulders. Tom staggered, then steadied himself, and began to walk. Creep hopped along beside him, putting his hands up to the ends of the rods, trying to keep them from slipping and pulling Tom sideways and over. And so they went along.

They went through narrow alleys of stinking mud; past tumbledown soot-caked walls, sheds with cracked roofs, little gates into dirty yards, and everywhere past chimneys, and the endless sound of hammers ringing on metal, clanging and jangling like thousands of cracked church-bells gone mad.

Then they came to a narrow way between the backs of two rows of houses. Right and left were nailors shops, little lean-to sheds against the back walls of the rows. At the door of one of these black dens they stopped. And from within came the sound of singing. Over the crash and ring of the hammer, over the rapid ding-dong-ding of a hand hammer, over the roar of a fire, a little sweet voice reached them, singing:

"If I were a blackbird, I'd whistle and sing,
"I'd foller...."

Looking within, Creep saw a fire on a raised hearth. Iron rods lay like red weals across the ashes of the hearth; a woman at an anvil plied a hammer, stooped over her task, with her face lit from below in the glow of the forge. And behind and above her, hanging on a loop of sooty rope from the roof-tree a little girl dangled, one foot on a cross beam, and the other treading up and down on a bellows-handle, to blow the fire to furnace heat. Round the yellow-gold of her head of tousled hair flew hundreds of red sparks in the updraught of hot air, like a swarm of fireflies, enveloping her, and she was singing as she worked.

"Stop that caterwauling, and save thy breath for thy work, else I'll punch thee up the throat!" said the man. He took the load off Tom's back, and stacked the iron in a corner. The woman did not stop working, but kept her eyes on the man with a dog-like look in her eyes. He gave her a coin from his pocket. She glanced at it, put it in her apron, and laying down her hammer went out, without a word.

The man lifted the little girl down from her perch, and told Tom to get up there in her place. She staggered across the floor, as though her legs were uneven in length from standing so long upon one and working so hard with the other. She cast a long look out of the open door, her eyes widening as she saw Creep, looking in. But the man seized her, roughly, and set her standing on a wooden box beside the anvil; she would not have been tall enough to reach from standing on the floor.

Creep watched. The man chopped up rods of iron with a heavy hammer fixed to his bench, and cast the pieces in handfuls in the fire. Then he cried, "Blow!" to Tom, and as Tom trod the bellows, and the fire flared up, he pulled out the red-hot lengths with a pair of tongs, and passed them to the girl. And she put them in another pair of tongs across her anvil, and laid over them a tool like a mallet, with a curved head, held in her left hand, and with her right hand she beat the back of this tool with a heavy hammer. The glowing worm of metal twisted round into a loop, and she cast it back into the fire. Then the man drew it forth again, once more red-hot and blazing, and hooked it first through the end of a long chain hanging from the anvil, and then over a snib on the anvil, and hammered the two hot ends together to form a solid link. And then they began again, and again, again, again....

In a while the man took off his apron, and threatening to belt Tom and the girl if the chain was not a hundred links longer when he returned, he went out, leaving her to make the links all by herself.

"Who's that?" she said, when his footsteps had died out of hearing, pointing at Creep with a pair of tongs.

"That's Creep," said Tom. "He's with me."

"There won't be neither work nor food for him here," said the girl. "And there won't be much for us, either, Whatever-you're-called. They'll have drunk most to the last penny before they thinks of our supper."

"I'm Tom," said Tom.

"Blow, can't yer!" the girl replied. She wiped the sweat from her forehead with the back of her sooty hand, and began to batter out another link. Creep sidled up to her, watching. Then he reached out a thin hand and held the shaping tool for her, leaving her two hands free to swing the hammer.

"Tha'd better tell thy friend he won't get paid," she said. "He's helping me with the dolly for a bellyful of air!"

"You let him," said Tom, "if he wants to. He's a touch odd, our Creep."

"Simple, you mean? Christ love us, how's he going to do here?"

"No," said Tom. "He in't simple. Not that at all ..." And all the while Tom thrust the bellows down with

56

his foot, and a weight on a pulley lifted them open again. And the little girl on her box pulled the iron in and out of the fire, and beat the dolly with her hammer, and Creep stood beside her, helping with his bony hands. They sweated, and clean rivulets striped their cheeks and grimy arms. And by and by the little girl began to sing again, breathlessly, in little broken phrases between hammer blows:

"*If I was a blackbird ... I'd whistle and sing ...*

"*I'd foller the barge ...* I wouldn't stay *here*," she added under her breath, as they heard footfalls coming down the yard.

6

Christopher woke feeling he must be drowning—seeing the wavering nets of watery light just above his head. Then he saw he was lying in a narrow bunk, under a striped blanket, and the light was cast off the water outside onto a white cabin roof through a window at his side. He travelled the day before in his mind's eye, taking time to remember where he had got to. At last he recalled the plate of bacon and egg, and the warm boat yesterday evening, and so came home to himself, and remembered where he was.

He swung his feet over the side of the bunk, and sat up, knocking his head. A narrow gangway down the boat led him to a tiny kitchen, where breakfast was laid on a counter with three stools. "Feeling better?" said the woman, smiling, and pouring him a mug of coffee. The man put down his book.

"Got lost yesterday, I suppose. There'll be people out looking for you. Someone worried out their mind, I'm sure. So how did you come to be under a bridge miles from anywhere? Tell us your name and address."

"I can get home on me own, now it's light," said

Christopher. "They won't be looking for me, honest."

"Done it before then, have you?" said the man. "But for all your people know you've been out in the open all night. We think we ought to take you safely home, right away."

Christopher said nothing, and bit his lip.

"Well, have something to eat first," said the woman. "Do you like porridge with syrup? And we'll work out what to do about you after." She put a pretty blue bowl in front of him, with a spiral of syrup melting into hot porridge. She smiled at him; but she also caught the man's eye with an urgent secret message in her glance.

Christopher ate. The two adults spread a map out and began to discuss the day's trip. "If we get going soon, and keep at it, and if it doesn't take too long to see this young man home," the man said, "we should be through the grim bit by tonight. Open country again by tomorrow."

"Does that allow time for some shopping? We need cheese, and soap."

"A bit of time. Not half the morning, love, unless you want to be tied up in a slum overnight."

"Where does this lot go, then?" said Christopher, suddenly interested.

"This lot?"

"Canals and that."

"Where do you want to go? Brummagem, Manchester, Liverpool, London, Leeds? It goes most places."

"Not as many as it used to go to, though," said the woman, leaning over the map. "There used to be miles and miles more. Look, here, for example, is a branch line that isn't navigable any more. You must

59

have passed it, coming this way yesterday. Perhaps you didn't notice?"

"Oh, yes," the man said. "Quite hard to see, till you get an eye for them. It's a good one, that one. Had inclined planes instead of locks. But it's a lost cause. Getting all built over by new town houses. Too late to save that one, I'm afraid."

Christopher looked at them, baffled. But an urgent idea filled his mind. If there was a fork in the canal, a branch, then perhaps he had failed to find Creep because Creep had followed the branch, and he himself had gone straight on. That would explain it! It would explain both how Creep seemed to have got so impossibly far, and why he kept having that funny feeling that he had somehow overtaken Creep, that Creep was somehow behind him. All he had to do now was to escape from all this worried kindness—they were probably going to take him to a police station!— and then go and find that turning.

He ate slice after slice of toast, doggedly stuffing himself, and kept his eye on the boat. Beyond the kitchen was a long cabin with seats and cushions, and at the far end of that was a door into the front cockpit. When the man got up to take his dirty plate to the sink, Christopher had nothing between him and the door; he jumped up, and ran down the boat through the door, and up onto the front deck, and in a flying leap from there on to the towpath. He ran for the bridge as fast as he could go, and then turned and yelled, "Thanks! Tara, then!" and ran on. They were calling after him, and the man was pulling boots on, ready to come after him. He had the sense to realise they wouldn't want to leave the boat, so he ran across the bridge, and away from the canal, making for a small spinney on the skyline that looked good enough to hide in.

When he reached it he lay down in the deep grass at the edge of the trees, and looked back across the open field to the canal. The man was standing on the bridge, calling. Birdsong overhead cut through his distant voice. He did not come up the slope. Christopher lay still, and waited till he heard the *putter putter* of the boat's engine, and saw its red and green cabin sides moving along the bottom of the field. The woman at the tiller was looking his way, anxiously scanning the field with a hand raised to shade her eyes from the morning sun.

Christopher lay quite still and watched the boat out of sight. Then he got up, and trotted back to the canal. He began to retrace his steps of the day before, dodging round gaps in the towpath, doggedly pushing through nettles and thorns, ignoring the scratches and stings on his bare legs. The water of the cut stretched before him, double green; green itself with a dim grey-green of water full of living things, and brightly splashed with green light from sunlit reflected trees in the air above. A rich June juicy emerald colour spread everywhere, and the creamy cow-parsley frothed and bubbled along the hedgerows and in the towpath grasses, and weighed the air with its sweet sleepy stench.

He had been going for some time when he caught a glimpse of movement in the grass, a blue patch, the shape of a small figure sitting in the hedge.

"Creep!" he cried, running forward with a thumping heart, "Creep?" But it was only Pauline, sitting by the cut, tipping specks of gravel out of her plimsolls.

"Where you bin all night?" she demanded, looking up. "She ain't half in a state! And it ain't fair, leaving me to cop it for you."

"Well, you told her, didn't you? Din't you tell her where I was?"

"Bloody wish I hadn't told her!" said Pauline. "She made a real old carry on; screaming off about you bein' by the cut in the dark by yourself. Then I told her you wasn't by yourself, 'cos you'd have found Creep by now, and then she stopped and changed her mind quick about calling the police. Then today she said I wasn't to go to school, I was to come and get you home. You better come quick, Chris."

"I'm not going home without Creep."

"But he might of fell in the cut and drowned hisself or anything might've happened to him. You might look for days and not find him. Come on."

"He's my brother, Pauline, don't you see? And he's *yours*, too!"

"Well, it don't feel like that, do it? And anyway, he's only half."

"What do you mean, half?"

"Well, he had a different dad, while ours was away, din't he; and I s'pose his dad was mean with our mum, and that's why she don't like Creep."

"But ... but our dad hadn't gone off when ... when she got Creep, Pauley. I remember him coming to see us after there was Creep. He brought me a clockwork parrot, and you a doll, and...."

"And he saw Creep, and he hasn't been home since," said Pauline. "You may be older'n me, Chris, but you're simple, that's what!"

"Anyway, whatsit matter who his dad was? He's still our brother."

"I don't want a brother what isn't one really, and what's always snivelling, and what smells! I don't want him! I wish he wasn't there. I wish he hadn't *never* been there!" She rubbed away tears, her knuckles pressed in her eyes.

"Now you're bawling," said Christopher. "I don't understand you. Why you bawling, if you don't want him back?"

"Well, you won't come home, and I'm going to catch it if I go back without you, ain't I?"

"All right then, I'll come home. And then I'll have to go and tell the Cruelty man, and ask him to find him."

"No!" screamed Pauline. "No, Chris, we musn't! We musn't never tell the Welfare, or the Cruelty nothink about it. If we do, they'll lock her up!"

"Is that what she told you?" asked Chris.

Pauline nodded, sniffling.

"Well then you see, someone's got to care about him, Pauley, and the only someone there is is me. And if you don't want to go home by yourself, you'll have to stop with me till we find him."

"Will you do my laces for me, then?"

"All right. Put your foot up."

"And piggyback me over all that mud?"

"All right. All right...."

When they found the canal branch he wondered how he hadn't seen it before. An arc of cast iron took the towpath up and over it. Below the towpath bridge it lay blocked off with some baulks of wood. Behind the blockage the water was thick with waterlily leaves, and reeds, and a curdled skin of floating rubbish. The towpath of the branch was heavily overgrown, but, Chris noticed, looking down on it from the bridge, someone had passed that way, for the grass was trodden down, the milky stems of the dandelions were crushed and oozing. He broke a thick stick from the hedge, to help clear their way, and they went on.

The line of the branch swung away from the main canal and hugged close along the bottom of a wood. After the wood it crossed an embankment, high above fields to left and right. They could see a long distance, and could make out, from a pair of distant tumbledown bridges, the direction they were about to take. Stopping on the bank, cupping his hands round his mouth, Christopher yelled, "Creep! CREEP!" across the green field, shimmering with windsilk below him. Then, straining to hear any answer, however faint or far, he became aware of larks, one near, several further off, trilling keenly overhead in the wide sky. But no answer came. Half a mile further he tried again, and again heard the silence full of small sounds—a bee purring, a small creature splashing softly in the water of the cut.

The cut had become very narrow. It was constricted by the brigades of rushes wading into it from either bank. Yellow and white flowers grew in it. The water was crystal clear, and in its glassy shallows deep weed forests could be seen, and the shadow lines of little fishes. The bridges over it were broken, and, where a lane came near, the cut was full of rubbish: a pram frame, a mattress all springs and stuffing scattered around, old oil drums, blue plastic bags. Then the canal turned away from the lane, and the rubbish petered out.

Pauline was getting hot, trailing far behind Christopher, moaning at him that she was tired. He was hot himself. They had come a long way, and

Pauline's way from home had been even longer for a little kid.

"All right," he said. "We'll rest for a bit." He sat down on the path, took his socks and plimsolls off, and dangled his feet in the cool water. He dipped his hands, and splashed his face, but he didn't like to drink any.

Pauline, coming up to him, didn't sit and rest. She saw a butterfly, and began to chase it, and then began to pick a bunch of flowers. It seemed, as soon as they stopped, she wasn't so tired after all.

A duck skid-landed on the water near Christopher, and at once was driven off by two earlier arrivals, with much creaking quacking, and beating of wings.

Christopher got up, and sighed. He called Pauline. She was slow coming back. He put his filthy socks in his pocket, put his plimsolls back on wet feet, and with his sister still lagging behind him, walked on.

7

The little girl was wrong, as it happened, about supper. The footfalls in the yard were those of the woman returning. She set a jug and bowl down at the door, and called to the children to come and take it.

"Come on down, then, Tom-noddy!" the girl called.

"You watch who you're calling what!" said Tom, jumping down, and staggering with the same uneven gait that she had shown when first lifted down from the bellows. "And what are *you* called, then?"

"My name is Lucy," she said, "but I'm always called Blackie."

They went outside, and sat down upon a bundle of rods. There was a mess of something in the bowl, and a small sup of beer remaining in the jug.

"What have we got?" said Tom, peering into the bowl.

"Taturs and bacon."

"Thowt you said as us'd get nowt."

"There'll be nowt tomorrow, on account of this," said Blackie with a sigh. "Next to nowt till next week come payday."

A beam of sunshine struck down through the murky dirty air of the yard, and she turned her head.

"Gawd help us!" cried Tom in dismay. "You look horrible, Blackie! What happened to yer?" For he had just seen the side of her face that had been turned away from the light while she worked. A huge crinkled pink and black scar lay across her visage; her mouth was pulled crooked at the corner, her eye was drawn tight and half shut, and her eyelashes were gone.

"I fell asleep at the bellows," she said. "I fell forward into the fire. Well," she added, as though he had accused her of stupidity, "he won't let me sing to keep myself awake, see? You'll have to mind yourself, Tom."

Tom had not taken his eyes off her face. "Why is it *black*?" he asked, his voice rising and squeaking slightly.

"The skin's growed over the coal dirt from the fire," she said, sadly. "It hurt too much to wash it off," she added. "Aren't you ever going to stop gawking and eat up? You in't such a picture yourself!" She picked up the bowl, and took the tin spoon. "Three ways?" she said, beginning to draw a line across the surface.

"I don't want none," said Creep, who had sat down on her ugly side. "You have it."

"You can't have *none*," she said. "You'll be hungry, you silly bugger!"

"I'm not hungry," said Creep.

"You must be," said Tom. "You didn't have nothing at all for as long as you've been with me."

"Can't seem to get up an appetite, can't yer?" said Blackie, with a soft note in her voice. "Course it isn't real nice food, but it's what we got."

Creep just shook his head at her.

"You don't want to worry about us," she coaxed. "Look, there's quite a bit here. Tom's a big boy, ever so strong, he looks. And I looks little and peaky, I know, but then I'm not very old, see? I'm only going on eight. How big would you think I'd be, at eight? You're the smallest; you needs your share!" And when Creep still pushed the bowl aside she said crossly, "Didn't your mam make you sup your snap?"

"No," said Creep. "She never. Me brother did. He brought me what he had over, see, and got me to eat it. She didn't care!"

"Oh," said Blackie. "You poor perisher!"

"Sorry, Creep," said Tom suddenly. "Can't argue no longer," and he took the bowl from Blackie's hands, drew a line across the middle, and began to eat.

"That brother," said Blackie, eyeing Tom's progress through the taturs, "you mean just what he got for himself would do for you too? Love us! Where is he now?"

"Don't know," said Creep. "He might be looking for me, though."

"You ought to leave a mark to help him find you. Where will he be looking?"

"Up the cut," said Tom. "We come on Creep's boat."

"It isn't mine," said Creep. "I just found it."

Blackie took the bowl from Tom, and began to eat.

At that moment the man came back into the yard. He was carrying a bundle of thick rods, and a curious piece of finished chain in his right hand.

"Up off yer backside, and get blowing!" he said curtly to Tom. "I've got an extra job to bring me a bit o' money, and it's to be done right away!"

Tom got up, and scrambled up to his perch. Blackie ran to put more coals upon the furnace, and rake it over, for it had died down to a soft glow while they were supping. The man put on the bench in front of him a length of chain with a huge flattened link on it every yard or so. These big links were made with a slot and a loop so that they could be padlocked.

"Like that," the man said. "A dozen like that, by the morning. I'll make the collars, and you put the chain links on them, Blackie."

"I'm tired," she said.

"Bloody hell, so am I!" said the man. And he began working.

Blackie began, too, drawing the hot lengths from the fire, bending and hammering them, but her hammer strokes limped, and rang unevenly. The work went slowly. The thick rod had to be heated right through till it blazed white, and then beaten flat with a big treadle hammer on the bench. The strip was then bent round in a ring, and the bellows were wanted going fiercely all the time.

"I don't like making these," said Blackie, wailing above the racket of hammering and the roar of the fire.

"Quit mauthering," said the man. "T'ain't for thee to wear them."

"For me to make them, though," she said. "They make my heart stop to think on. Can we not even put more links between one man and the next, gaffer?"

"And lengthen our labour, for the same money?" he cried.

"Oh, could we not—" she began.

At that the man, drawing a freshly heated iron bar from the fire, shook the shower of sparks and fragments that flew from it not on the floor but over Blackie, saying, "Get *on*, will yer?"

Blackie danced up and down, wailing, shaking the

hot sparks out of her hair, and out of her smock where they had lodged against her skin. And Tom, dangling above her with his arms aching and his legs numb, had suddenly a memory of the pock-marked skin of Blackie's arms and legs, and understood. He was too afraid for himself to stop working.

"Can't we finish in the morning, gaffer?" said Blackie some long time later.

"These must be ready to go down to Bristol at daybreak, Blackie," said the man wearily. "Sorry, hen. You can nap the morning out, I daresay." He sounded mild. But later, when she was nodding, and missing her target with one blow out of two, he shouted at her again, and swung the swarm of sparks at her to wake her. This time Creep stepped in front of her, silently, and the sparks fell over him. Then he, too, danced, shaking the cruel scraps off, slapping his scorched rags to stop them smouldering, and whimpering a little. And the man stared, and frowned, and wiped his eyes with the back of his hands, and then went on working.

A thin pale dawn was leaching the sky behind the chimneys of the facing row, when suddenly it was done. The man took the last chain, and put it into a bucket of water, where it exploded, hissing ferociously with steam, and emitted a kettle smell. It was still too hot to carry when he drew it forth, so he wrapped it in rag, and then took it up with the others across his shoulders, and without a word to them, staggered out with their night's work.

"I'm going from here, Creep," said Tom, when the three of them stood in the yard, leaning up on the wall for strength to stand. "What use to run from the mine, and come to this?"

"All right," said Creep.

"Will thy boat take us somewhere else away, dost tha think?"

"Dunno. Could."

"Shall us find our road back to it, then?"

"All right," said Creep. "Blackie too."

"Do you want to come, Blackie?" said Tom doubtfully.

Her face was indecipherable in the gloom, but her voice lit up. "*Would* you tek me? Would you truly?"

"Don't you mind leaving your father'n mother?" said Tom.

"Them's not me father'n mother!" she said scornfully. "Me mam sold me to 'em for ten shilling, last winter."

"I don't know," said Tom. "I always used to think if I had only a mother, how better I would be. Used to lie awake in the poor house, making me a mother in me mind. But you two...."

"Well, if we're going anywhere, Tom-noddy," said Blackie, "start walking while it's yet dark; they'll be after us!"

So the three crept out of the yard, and down winding alleys. They staggered along, groaning with weariness, and found at last a bunch of dirty bushes beside the road out of town. By this time Tom was almost carrying Blackie, asleep on her feet, so they crept in behind the leaves, curled up like three kittens one upon another, and fell asleep.

Mid morning sounds woke them. The light filtered down through the dirty leaves, and speckled their faces. Carts were rumbling by along the road. Tom stood on the dusty verge, and hailed passing carts, asking for a ride to "the place where the iron rods are made", saying he had to go and bring a load for his master. They were lucky: an empty cart stopped for him. Blackie and Creep slipped up beside him. The carter was a sun-tanned man with pale grey eyes beneath bushy brows.

"How many is it?" he asked Tom.

"Three. I mean two...." Tom corrected himself.

The carter stared long at Creep. "Split the difference. Call it two and a half," he said. "Hop in, then."

So towards evening they were put down outside the row of nailers' cottages by the river below the furnace valley, and they walked up past the roaring and blazing and smoking ironworks, to the canal winding along the wooded heights above. And there was Creep's boat, just where they had left it. The woods were green around it, and birds were singing. Together Tom and Creep pulled it a bit further, out of the light of the foundry, into the shade of the trees, and up to a bridge. And Blackie danced about, laughing, saying, "Oh in't it lovely, in't it green!" Then, when she caught a glimpse of herself in the water, she said, "I'd like a clean pinafore, more than anything!"

"More than a hot dinner, Blackie? More than a new face?" said Tom, grinning.

"More than a mother, Tom-noddy!" she flashed, and that silenced him.

"Don't the air taste nice to breathe, up here," she said in a while. "Was you going to put your mark somewhere, Creep, to help your brother find you?"

"I'd like to," said Creep, "but I don't know how."

"I could show you your name," said Blackie.

"Can you *write*?" said Tom, staring at her.

"Only a bit. Me grandad taught me me letters. I could do his name."

"All right," said Tom. "Let's see you." He picked up a piece of chalky stone, and gave it to her.

"On the bridge then," she said. "Anybody would see it there," and she chose a large well-squared block of stone built into the spring of the arch on the bridge where it curved up to span the towpath, and on the surface facing down the path she wrote *CREEP* in large, wobbly letters.

"How do I know that's right?" said Tom.

"If you could write, you'd know it was," she said, proudly.

"Trouble is," said Tom, "that'll wash off when it rains. We'd better cut it in a bit."

Creep fetched some scrap iron from the rubbish in his boat, and Tom sharpened the ends on the stonework of the bridge and gave them one apiece. They began to scratch round the outlines of the letters. At first it seemed impossible; then they began to make grooves in which the iron could run and slide, and the grooves deepened steadily.

"Where are we going, Creep, when we've done this?" said Tom in a while.

"I met a girl from a pottery once," said Blackie, "When I was buying taturs. She had a clean apron, and nice hands. She said she put lines and flowers on cups and that. I'd like work like that."

"We could try," said Tom, finishing the curve of C, "if we knew where a pottery is."

"Could we really try?" said Blackie.

"Come on, then," said Creep, throwing his scraper in the water, as he finished P.

They stood back to admire their work. "That'll do," said Tom. "That'll last us out." Then they got on to the boat, and, as though it had heard their talk, it began to move. It glided on through the bridge, and round a smooth bend. The water chuckled gently under its blunt front end.

"It's good the way it goes, in't it?" Creep said, idly dangling four cool fingers in the water. But beside him the other two were fast asleep.

8

Christopher's damp toes squelched in his soggy plimsolls. The going got harder; the towpath hedge had grown over the path, and it was a thickset hedge of blackthorn, armed with long prickles. Pauline got crosser and crosser. He kept having to carry her, piggyback, or stop to unhook strands of her hair from the thornbush. The canal wound its way into a wood, past a derelict brick building with a fallen roof and two tall chimneys. Then it wound into woodland again. On one side, towards the crest of the slope, fields full of thick gold buttercups could be seen; on the other, the ground sloped away below close-crowded trees. There were many bridges over the canal, made of rosy faded brick but the arch and parapet edged with pale creamy blocks of stone. Below, in the mirror world, another arch completed the circle. Christopher kept going, with Pauline dragging after him, for the lush growth on the path was still beaten down flat in front of him. Somebody had been this way not long ago.

At last he stopped. Pauline was far behind; he would have to wait for her to catch up. He had stopped beside one of the bridges, in a shady spot. From what he could see, Pauline seemed to be picking flowers again; she had thrown away the first bunch, because it had drooped in her hands. Christopher sighed. He hadn't the energy to go back and chivvy her, instead he lay down full length in the grass by the bridge, and rested. He looked straight up into the sky. Tears pricked his eyes. He knew really that he had to go home. He couldn't keep going for ever, and he supposed he had lost Creep now for good.

He thought of home without Creep; just ordinary, like other people's. "We could eat all our chips ourselves. ..." Pauline had said. But she was too young to understand. Just getting rid of Creep wouldn't make things right. He didn't want home without Creep. And Creep had gone....

A swallow swam across his vision, swooping a lovely curve across the sky. Turning his head to follow its movement, Christopher suddenly saw something on the side of the bridge. He sat up abruptly, staring, and with the hair on his scalp tingling. One of the stones of the bridge arch had been marked; written on. In crooked, large letters, scratched in a wavering shallow groove, the stone said *CREEP*.

Christopher stared, his head swimming. At the corner of the stone the letters had been nibbled away by some deep furrows, running along the surface that faced the canal. Three inches deep and more, one above the other, they were scored sharply into the fabric. One of them had cut the capital *C* on *CREEP* into two separate half moons. And then a black iron bar had been put onto the corner angle, and that, too, was deeply notched and grooved.

Christopher was trembling as he stared. A voice above his head said, "Curious old stone, that, isn't it?"

making him jump out of his skin. Looking up he found himself looking into the pale grey eyes of a workman, who was leaning over the parapet of the bridge.

Christopher said, "How long has *that* been there?"

"Hundred and fifty year?" the other speculated.

"No!" said Christopher. "It can't have!"

"Just look at it," said the man, coming down from the bridge, and standing beside the boy. "It's part of the arch, see? Got to be as old as the bridge, hasn't it?"

"But the writing! The writing could be new! The writing could've been done yesterday, couldn't it?"

"Not very well," said the man. "You look at it, son. There's moss in it, there's bits of lichen. And then look at those grooves. Done after the writing, those were, because they've nipped the front end off the first letter, ain't they?"

"Yes," said Christopher, wildly.

"Know what made them grooves, do yer, boyo?"

"No."

"Horses. That's what."

"*Horses?*"

"Tow-ropes. When the barges were pulled by horses, see, and the ropes ran along and snagged the corners of the bridge. That's what the iron's for—to keep the ropes from biting the bridge to bits. And they made a fair old mark on the iron, too, see? A wet rope with a bit of grit from the path on it, good as a file for grinding!"

"But ..."

"Mind you, there haven't been any horses along here for a while. 1948 the last load came up to the mill here, and that was a motor boat. I can just remember the horses from when I was a lad smaller than you."

"Oh, something's *wrong. Wrong*!" cried Christopher, in panic.

"Just neglect. That's what. Nobody giving a damn what happened to it all. It's just left to rot away. The boaties have all got cottages. Some of us works as lock-keepers, helping the toy boats through. They're going to clean this lot out up to the next bridge by next year; that's why we're driving piles up there. Then there'll be plastic boats down this way, too. Better than nothing. But the day I see a horse draw a loaded pair this way again, I'll buy the world a pint!"

"You're wrong!" said Christopher, turning a face all puckered and taut towards the man. "You've got to be wrong! He hasn't been gone more than a day!"

"You feeling all right, son?" said the man. "What are you on about?"

But Christopher suddenly ran. Creep had been there; Creep had left a sign; Creep *wanted* to be found; he must be just a little way further ahead, just a little way on.

Forgetting Pauline, Christopher ran. First he passed a working gang, driving in steel plates to mend the crumbled towpath. They were sitting on their punt-shaped boat, eating bread and cheese. The man at the bridge must have been one of them. Then he passed a strange sort of brick structure beside the cut. Glancing right as he passed it he saw a huge long slope descending at a smooth angle through the trees, making a long green grassy incline. At the bottom a bridge crossed it, and he had a glimpse of brown water.

Then he came to a line or two of little red terraced cottages, and beyond them a huge building in red and yellow brick, with line upon line of windows, and a tall round chimney. In patterns of brick and tile this building declared TRIUMPHANT to the world, but a tattered painted board fixed lower down said *Storage and Warehousing*. Beside it another sign said TO LET in faded paint. There was no sound or sign of movement. A wide wharf fronted the canal alongside this place, but, Christopher suddenly realised, there was no water. The silted shallows he had walked beside were all dried up here, and only a pool of clotted mud in the bottom of the canal bed remained. There was a wire fence along the brink, and a sign on it said *No Entry*. It didn't look like a place Creep could have run to earth and hidden in. Christopher ran on.

There was no path any more; he ran in the dry green bottom of the canal, with tall banks on either side of him masking the view. Little trees had taken root down there, and a few marshy reeds in boggy patches. It was hard going. The scrubby bushes got thicker, and he had to push and thrust through them. Suddenly, in the depth of a thicket, he came to another kind of obstacle. The corpse of a broken and rotting boat lay there, half hidden. It was a simple flat-boat, like the one the workmen at the bridge had been using, but it was rusted into flaking holes all over. The cabin sides were perished; a hole yawned in the cabin top where a chimney had gone through. A rubble of rusting iron lay on the cabin floor. Christopher climbed into the boat, and sat down on the pile of iron. He felt suddenly calm.

He did stand up and yell, "CREEP!" to the birds and bushes around him, but he hardly bothered to listen for a reply. He remembered again a neighbour's voice, tight and shocked, saying, "If I knew that was still happening, I'd have to report it. It's like going right back to the bad old days!"

"I know what happened to you, Creep," Christopher said, softly and sadly. "But how do I look for you, *now*?"

9

Creep, too, was asleep when the boat stopped again. And so it was in the light of early morning that they saw the new place it had chosen for them. There was an engine house beside the cut, a little way ahead of them. A long train of tub-boats full of coal was tied up, blocking the way past, and as the three children, rubbing their eyes and yawning, watched, two of these boats were suddenly lifted out of the water on a trolley, and disappeared from view, moving sideways.

"Eyup!" said Tom, and he began to scamper along the towpath towards the mysterious building. The others followed.

What they saw was astonishing. The boats that had just been drawn up sideways out of the water were now halfway down the hillside, travelling slowly on rails, lowered away by unwinding chains. And on parallel rails ascending came two others.

The slope was very long and steep; and across the bottom of it stretched a little bridge, beyond which lay the green-brown waters of the river, and the sloping wooded opposite shore.

They lingered, staring. When the rising tub-boats

reached the top of the long incline they slid over a hump, and down a short reverse slope into the canal. The trolley that carried them sank into the water, and the boats were floated off, and drawn away by a boatman waiting with a horse.

"Look what's in them!" said Blackie, suddenly. For the boats were just moving past them. They were full of sawdust, and in the sawdust they could see the nearly buried shapes of jugs and bowls.

"Are you admiring my lovely engine, then, my ducks?" said a man suddenly emerging from the winding house. He had coal dust all over his arms and apron, and had obviously been stoking the boiler that ran the steam engine that worked the movement of boats on the slope. "Now what do you think of my marvellous jenny, and her long incline?"

"I'm boggled at it, sir," said Tom.

"And well you might be, young man; I'm glad to hear it of you! Not a drop of water lost; better than locks, eh? Coal goes down all day, and pots come up, and the water all stays where it is. Wonder of the age, this is! And where would it be without I kept it stoked up with a head of steam to keep it driving smoothly?"

"Where do the pots come from, sir?" asked Blackie.

"The pottery down below. You can walk down and see it, if you've a mind to. But keep yourselven well clear of the moving chains!"

"Thank you," said Tom, and they skipped off, and began the descent. They slipped and slid on the grass beside the rails, and laughed as they went. Or at least, Blackie laughed, and Tom did. Creep only smiled, and that rather carefully, as though his cheeks might crack.

When they reached the bridge that carried a lane over the bottom of the incline, they could see the pottery. It was a jumbled cluster of buildings, and among them several kilns—like huge blackened bottles built of brick, standing up above the workshop roofs, and pouring out smoke from their narrow necks. A little bell swung on a rope above the roof, and this now began to ring. People came out of the cottages by the river side, and clattered across the bridge, past the children. They nodded and chattered to each other as they flowed through the gate.

"Come on, then," said Tom. "Let's see if they'll have us."

There was a porter at the gate. Blackie and Creep hung back, but Tom went boldly up to him, and asked if there was work for a stout lad. "Wait on," said the porter, when he had looked Tom over hard. Then he called someone over to him from the workshop door across a little yard, and asked about Jonas' boy. Soon Jonas himself came to look at Tom. "You look strong enough," he said. "You can run moulds for me for a week or two, if you like, while my boy mends. He's poorly. I'll set you on, and see how you go."

"What about my ... my sister?" said Tom, pointing at Blackie.

"She can turn for me. Three shilling a week for the both of you, if you work fair and steady."

"I can work fair, master, if I'm shown the way of it," said Tom.

"Look well, then, while I show thee," said the other. And while Creep stepped along unseen beside the other two, they followed Jonas across the brick-paved yard, under the shadow of the tall bottle-shaped towers, into a room in a workshop. The shop was small; it was dirty with a white dirt everywhere. A window of small panes looked through a screen of trees at the rapid brown river surging by. There was a device with wheels and a drive-belt standing within, and a bench, and tubs of clay.

"Wedging first," said Jonas. He scooped a mass of clay out of a barrel at the door, and put it on the bench. Then he cut it in two, by drawing a wire through it, took up the one half of the mass, and raising it high above his head, slapped it down upon the other half, making them one again. "Thus," he said, again cutting it up, "and thus!" knocking it together again. "Now you."

Tom began to work the clay. It had to be heaved high and smashed down again over and over before Jonas was satisfied. Slowly it softened, and seemed to wetten, turning like putty.

"Right," said Jonas at last. "Now balling. The wench can help with this."

The sweat was running freely off Tom's brow, as he learned the next task. This was cutting the clay into small lumps of equal size, so that Blackie could roll them round the bench and make them into balls, which Jonas took up and rolled out flat like pancakes. "These are battings," Jonas told them. "When we've enough battings made up, we'll go to moulding."

So when the battings were all made ready, Jonas took a mould of plaster, and set it on his wheel, and dipped his right hand in a bowl of water. Then he bade Blackie to wind hard on a handle that turned a wheel from which a belt spun his wheel, smooth and fast. With his left hand he put a batting down upon the spinning mould, and with his wet right hand he pressed it down. Then he took a wooden tool with a groove cut in it, and pressed it upon the turning clay, and the shape of the under side of a plate, with the rim it stands upon, sprung up from the clay. Then he cried "Stop!" to Blackie, and gave the mould with the plate upon it to Tom, and said, "Run thou now and set it in the drying room, and come again with another mould and make haste, or thou'lt hinder me."

"Where's the drying room, master?" said Tom.

"Why in the hovel, fule, where else would it be?" said Jonas, and then seeing Tom still baffled, he led him across the yard, into one of the bottle-buildings. "This is a hovel, boy; and within it is a kiln. This one doesn't get hot, just warm to dry the clay quickly on the moulds. Now you go in here ..." and he led the way into a brick room within the hovel, in the midst of which was an iron stove full of fire, with a chimney pipe glowing dark red with the heat, "... and you set the moulds on their edges, leaning upon these shelves and racks. When the lower shelves are full, you shin up those wooden steps to higher ones. And then, coming back you pick up an empty mould from the pile outside, and bring it on. Away wi' thee, then!"

Tom ran. Blackie watched him, coming with his shirt glued to his ribs with sweat, running in and out of the workshop, while she sat on a rickety stool, turning and turning the handle. Her lopsided face took on a more and more pathetic expression as he worked. Once she looked at him so keenly that she forgot herself, and wound her wheel so fast she set a plate spinning off the mould just as Jonas was about to make the foot-rim; and he shouted at her and promised to belt her if she did it again. Tom coming heard this, and stopped dead in the doorway, and got cuffed on the ear for delaying. In a while Creep slipped into the yard, and followed Tom into the hovel, and into the kiln. For a while he sat upon the step ladder, and took the moulds from Tom's hands, and himself set them on edge on the racks, so that Tom could turn at once upon his heels and run back again.

"You'll die roasted in here, Creep!" Tom said to him. "Come out of the heat, won't yer?" Creep did; but he didn't seem hot. He went and sat by a pile of moulds, and watched Tom's frantic passages across the yard. Then he went back within the shop and watched Blackie, turning her handle, and humming under her breath snatches of the tune she had sung in the forge. And by and by all the battings had been made up into plates, and by way of a rest Jonas set Tom to wedging another lump of clay.

When three times through they had worked this way, and the last mould was set in the heat, Tom had to bring them all out again, first in, first out, and return them to Jonas, one by one. And while Blackie kept the wheel spinning, Jonas "backed" the plates—polishing the surface smooth. And when each one had been burnished, Tom took it back to finish drying.

Then at last it was time for rest and food. The workers came out of the shops into the yards, and sat upon the steps, or in the grass along the river bank, and ate their modest food. Blackie and Tom were each given a crust of bread from some kind woman's kerchief, and a drink of sour beer by Jonas.

"You bring your own another time, mind," he said "We'll bide no begging here." Tom was so thirsty he crept back into the shop a moment, and drank the milky water that Jonas had wet his hands on to shape the clay. Someone called for Betty, asking her for a song, and a stout woman stood up and sang in a steady strong voice, while the men around her beat the time with their tin spoons on their cans.

> *"Though high flown folk may fall and break*
> *Yet we have ever yet been able*
> *To keep the wheelband i' the nick,*
> *Though often with a barish table...."*

"That's very moral, Betty," said Jonas. "Very fine. How about a gutsy ditty?"

"I wouldna sing your kind of song, Jonas, though you paid me for to," she replied, primly.

And then the bell rang, and everyone rose, and walked back through the gates to work again. What kind of song "Jonas' kind" might be would not appear that day.

When at last the day's task was all made up, late in the afternoon, the work changed. The plates were all dry enough to shell off the moulds, and only "fettling" them remained— smoothing off the flaws, and stacking them two dozen at a time in bungs, ready, Jonas told them, for the "firing" in another kiln the next day. And when all the fettling was done, Jonas took off his apron, and told Tom he must be there at six the next morning to light the stove in the drying room, and have it hot by seven, and Blackie must be there an hour after him.

So at last they three trailed home, up the long incline beside the boat lift, slow with fatigue. A rumbling pair of tub boats trundled down past them.

"You're shivering, Tom," said Blackie. "Are you well?"

"I'm right enough," he said. "But the air is cold after the stove down there."

"Shall us make us a fire to sit by?" she said. But when they reached the boat, tied up in the shelter of a willow tree, and seeming more tucked out of sight than when they had left it, only Creep had the strength to go about looking for kindling. He found some dry sticks, and then slid up to the engine house where the winding gear of the boat lift was driven, and stole a hot coal from the ashes raked out of the boiler there, to make it catch alight.

The iron stove in the boat cabin lit and burned brightly through its bars. Blackie made Tom sit almost on top of it so much did she care to have him warm. And when Creep whispered to her that perhaps something to eat would make him mend a little, she took an old tin can from the debris in the boat cabin, and stole away across the fields in the dark. When she came back she had the can full of milk, and two turnips in her apron pocket.

"That's stealing, Blackie," said Tom, looking with interest at her finds.

"Can't have the wolf full, and the sheep whole," she said.

"Who dost thou call a wolf?" he said. His voice was too weary to sound indignant. "Always calling names, you are. Right little gutterbug."

"It's a game for two, then, baint it?" she said. "Turnip seethed in milk for supper then. And don't tell me it's nasty, because I gotta eat it too."

Tom didn't say it was nasty. He ate it and sighed. Only when Blackie had eaten hers too, and licked her fingers rubbed all round the can, did she suddenly look up and say in a stricken tone, "Oh, Creep! I forgot to offer you none!"

"S'all right," said Creep. "I didn't want it."

10

"Why did you run away?" the woman asked. Her voice was kind in a business-like sort of way. On a desk in front of her lay a buff-coloured file.

"I was looking for my brother," Christopher said. She gazed at him, pursed lips, mentally taking notes. Pale; rather thin. Not undernourished. Shabby clothes, but clean, mended. A wary and hostile expression on his face, suspicious, untrusting. More than that, perhaps—actually burdened and harrassed like an adult. Like so many adults one saw....

"You haven't got a brother," she said.

"No," he said. "Not any more." His voice shook. "But I used to have."

The voice became very patient. The capable hand rang a bell in the desk. "No, Christopher. None of your neighbours ever saw a brother. The social worker who helps your family says there are just two of you, you and a sister, Pauline is she called?"

The door behind Christopher opened. He did not look round, but Pauline appeared beside him. "Here you are, Pauline," said the woman, smiling. "You see, Christopher, we have found your father, and he says he only has two children. Your mother says she had just you two. Let's see what Pauline says, shall we?"

Christopher said nothing. He bit his lower lip.

"Pauline, love, did you ever have a brother?"

The girl frowned, as though it were a hard question. "Someone like Christopher, you mean?" she asked.

"Yes; someone else like him."

"No," said Pauline. "There never was anyone like that."

"Now, Christopher," she said firmly, "why did you run away, really?"

"I was looking for my brother."

The woman frowned. Something here. Lying? No, not deliberately. Some emotional disturbance. If only there were more time ... but one saw too many cases, most of them worse. She looked in the file. The mother, she saw, was hard pressed, badly housed, deserted by the father, but doing her best. The child didn't truant from school, was not known to the police, was no bother in class....

"You weren't looking for anybody when you were found," she said. "You were hiding in a derelict boat."

"I was ... looking ... inside it, yes," said the boy carefully.

"Hiding," said the woman firmly. "And causing a lot of bother to other people. Worrying your mother, getting a lot of policemen looking for you, taking your sister far away from home, and then not even staying with her. It won't do, will it?" He was silent. "Well, Christopher, could you promise, do you think, that you won't run away like that again?"

There was a long silence. He did not meet her eyes.

"It would be easier for everyone if you could," she said gently.

"I won't do it again," said the boy flatly, defeated. "There isn't any point," he added, his voice suddenly full of a firmness to match hers. "He isn't here any more. He's gone back. There isn't any point in looking for him *now*."

"Are you very lonely?" she asked, making notes. "*Highly imaginative ... believes in a dream companion....*"

"Not really," said Christopher.

"You should try to make friends with some boys your own age, Christopher," she said. "You haven't got a brother."

"No miss," he said, suddenly docile.

She rang for someone to take them home. But she sat for a moment, puzzled, slightly troubled. "Better safe than sorry," she said to herself at last, and wrote "*Urgent, check*" across the section of the file marked *Number in family unit.*

11

One day working at the pot bank was much like another. The first comers to work, very early in the morning, were the little children. They came before the light to kindle the fires in the drying rooms. There was coal ready, piled damp and cold on the wharf by the river bank, for the master saw to that. As to dry sticks or ready sparks, that he did not trouble over, and the boys must find those for themselves. So they crept in and out of the hovels where the furnace mouths blazed red, spaced all round the bottom of the great firing kilns, and the firemen kept watch, ready to chase and beat any child they saw taking out a shovelful of fire; and yet till someone succeeded no new fires could be lit at all, and a beating from the mould-workers when they arrived loomed nearer and stiffened the courage of small creatures risking a beating from the firemen now.

Tom, at least, had Creep. Creep would gather kindling in the woods about the boat, and stack it to dry in the cabin ready, so that Tom could bring a handful each morning, and had not to go about to steal straw from the packing of barrels, or staves from crates for firewood. As for getting sparks, well, Tom would put his head in at the door of a hovel, and make a noise as though he was about to steal a hot coal, and Creep would slide by like a shadow, unseen as always, and come away with a trowel full of burnings held in a tin can under his rags, which nobody saw. Then when a fire was burning brightly in Tom's stove, he would let other less lucky boys take a light from it; any except Bill Wakes, whom he kept off, fighting him if need be, because Bill had tried to make Blackie tell him where she and Tom were dwelling, and had twisted her arm and made her cry when she would not say. The stolen fire made Tom king-cat until the grown-up workers arrived. Then he was just a runner, tearing through the rain, through the wind, into the heat of the hovel, and out again, a hundred and a hundred times a day.

It was summer; but it was a bleak and stormy one. Rain fell heavy and often, leaning out of a cold unseasonable wind that Tom learned to hate and dread.

Both Blackie and Tom learned Jonas as one learns the weather. When the work was behind he was angry, and cruel, dealing out blows and curses freely. When all was up to time he was calm and kind enough, and an easy master so long as they worked hard. He had his mother to keep, and a young wife and four children, of whom three were "mouths too small to work".

One day was much like another; but sometimes Jonas set Blackie to run errands for him, and so she visited the saucer square, the plate square, the china bank, the dipping shop, and learned her way through the huggermugger of workshops and kilns, the yards and stores, and learned the way of the clay, from the moulds or the throwing shop, dried, dipped in glaze, fired, painted and gilded, until, shining and ablaze with beauty it was muffled in straw and sawdust, and set forth into the world. She told the boys all about the in and outs of it as they climbed up the path by the incline each evening, looking sharp behind them in case Bill Wakes had the energy to follow, and spy upon them. Then they would sit upon the boat, eating their bite of supper, and talking, weariness making long silences between them, but the silence being full of kindness.

Blackie spent the money, buying bacon and taturs, and making them last. She bought needle and thread, and cobbled up the holes in their rags. She picked wilting handfuls of buttercups and comfrey along the canal bank, and set them in old tin cans in the cabin. The willow tree that leaned over the boat grew thick, and hung screens round it, making them a green and secret tent. Tom cleaned out the rusty cabin stove, and swept mounds of soot out of the chimney, making the fire draw well, and he bought an old mended pail from a tinker, so they had something in which they could set broth to warm. Creep cut bracken on the hillside, and made piles of it for them to sleep upon in the cabin. And so they got along. Once the fires were lit in the morning, Creep often slipped away back to the boat leaving the other two at work. He had watched a man fishing, and was determined to learn it. Blackie said you could eat fish, and though Creep took not a bite of food himself, he earned not a farthing either, and he wanted something to give Blackie when Tom so grandly gave his shillings over.

They got along; on Saturday Tom got paid, and Blackie went late to market. On Sundays they slept late, and then, for once not tired, not hungry, they talked and played. Tom had bought a handful of knuckle bones to play fives with, and though Blackie scolded him for wasting money she played with them just the same, indeed she usually won. Creep would smile and clap to see the stones fall out her way, but he laughed never, just as he never ate. Blackie called his smile a "Sunday face". "Look, Tom!" she would say. "Look at Creep; he's smiling, in't he?"

"Sort of," said Tom doubtfully.

"Let's make him laugh. Tell him summat funny, Tom." But either Tom didn't know anything funny, or he couldn't remember it when Blackie asked him.

So they lived day to day, Sunday to Sunday, and the green leaves on the wooded river banks, and round their boat, began to turn yellow, and a cold wind began to blow more days than not. A woman in the print shop gave Blackie an old shawl, and Blackie cut it up, and cobbled it together to make a waistcoat for Tom. He shivered a lot; and the colder the yard became across which he ran between workshop and kiln the worse his chills became. Creep wandered up and down the hillside, keeping a fire burning in the boat stove, and sitting on top of Tom's step ladder in the drying room, to take the moulds from him, and shorten his plunges into the choking heat-hardened air. The whole summer had a feeling of coming to an end.

Just the same, they were managing. One Sunday afternoon Blackie suddenly produced a little pot full of halfpennies and farthings, and began to count out her savings. "We need a blanket for the winter," she told Creep.

Tom said, "How could we get a blanket?"

"I'll think of something," said Blackie. "Perhaps I'll get paid a bit more."

"Thou'lt what?" said Tom.

"I might, so." she said. She paused. "Are you happy here, Tom?"

"Don't be daft," he said.

"Oh, Tom, you *will* be!" she said. "See, there's a place at t'other end of the pot bank, where they paint the best ware. Oh, Tom, it's lovely! They've a fire in there, just to keep them warm, and they sit at a table, with brushes and colours, and they have the pots ready with printed pictures, and they puts the red on the roses, and the green on the leaves, and lovely gold lines all round and round. And they sing while they work, there, or they have an old man reading to them out of a story book, to keep their minds content. You should just hear that story, Tom! It's about Christian, and Pilgrim, and ... well, see, I was taking a message in there, and I said, I just couldn't help myself, it came out, 'O,' I said, 'I'd fair like to work here!' And a woman looked up, and smiled at me, ever so pretty, and said, 'Little maid, can you draw a line straight as ninepence?' and I said, 'I've never seen ninepence, mum, but I'll try.' So she gave me her brush, and I took it, and put a line on a broken dish, and she was that surprised how I done it, she called the overlooker, and said, 'Look here,' and he said, 'Yes, well ...' and I think, Tom, they might let me go there, and draw the gold lines! And that rises up to ninepence a day, Tom, think on it!"

"How come you're so good at it, Blackie?" said Creep.

"I see them doing lines, always with one eye screwed up tight shut," she said. "And I've got one like that all the time, haven't I?"

"Good on you, Blackie!" said Creep, with his Sunday face.

"So, see, Tom," she went on, "I'll be a lady in the paintshop one of these next days, with a clean apron to put on, and you'll come up from mould-running to plate-maker, and then perhaps dipper; and we'll have us a little cot down by the river bank, and keep it swept ever so neat and clean. An' I'll cook thee thy supper, and mind the little ones...."

"Hang about!" said Tom, sitting up abruptly, and staring at Blackie. "What are you chuntering on about? What do you mean, little ones?"

Blackie said nothing, but looked at her reflection in the still water, and bit her lip.

"I'm not going ter marry you, Blackie," said Tom. "Doubt if *anyone*'ll marry yer; but I know *I* won't!"

Then Blackie jumped up, and ran away up the slope through the trees. In a while Creep walked after her, and came upon her lying face down upon a pile of russet leaves, crying bitterly. He sat beside her for a while, and put out a thin, grimy hand and touched her tousled golden hair, but she took no notice of him, and he soon crept away again.

He went back to the boat, and sat beside Tom. Tom was swinging his legs, kicking the side of the cabin, and whistling tunelessly between his teeth. He eyed Creep. Then, "It in't my fault, Creep, honest," he said.

Creep said nothing.

"When I get a girl," said Tom in a while, "she'll have a lovely kind face...."

"Blackie's kind," said Creep. Now Tom said nothing. "Couldn't you just sit on her good side, Tom? She looks quite all right, one way...."

"No!" said Tom. "No, I couldn't. Gives me the horrors every time she turns. An' where's she gone ramping off to? It's getting dark."

He was shivering again, and there were spots of high colour in his cheeks. "You go in, Tom," said Creep. "I'll get her."

He found her asleep on her leaves, her head cushioned on her arms. She said not a word when he woke her, nor a word to Tom when they closed the cabin door and lay down on their bracken beds; but in the morning she was up first, and singing, as she brought a can of stolen milk, taken from a sleepy cow in a dark field, to warm for Tom's breakfast.

And she was singing still when Creep and Tom set off to the works to get the fire lit.

They were down at the drying room at the usual time, or very near; but they found the fire lit already, and a big boy standing at the hovel door. He had a baulk of firewood in his hand, and he stood square and said to Tom, "S'all up wi' thee, unnerstand? I'm well now, and I'm having me job back!"

Tom stared at him. He had long since forgotten what Jonas had said about his regular boy being poorly. Creep whispered to him, reminding him.

"Got off with thee, then!" said the big boy, advancing a step, and swinging his piece of wood.

Tom stiffened, clenched his fists, and said steadily, "I'll not go till Jonas turns me off; and then I'll not go without a good part of this week's wages."

And as the big boy growled, and took another step forward, Tom's fists came up, and he said, "You'll have to fight to make me!" and at once a fireman put his head out from a hovel door across the yard, and bellowed at them.

"You don't fight here, hounds! You lay hands on each other and I'll have you both turned off."

And so the two of them stood, face to face, eyeing

each other, till Jonas came and hung his coat up behind the door.

"I'm sorry for it," he said to Tom. "And mayhap I'll regret it, one of these next days; but the job is promised to be back to him when he's well. I give my word, and I maun keep it."

Tom hung his head, and bit his lip; and just then there came Blackie into the yard, and behind her the overlooker in his worsted coat.

"What's about?" said the overlooker. Jonas told him "... an' he's a steady, strong enough lad," he finished, glancing at Tom.

"You," said the overlooker to Tom. "Step up here. Right. You can work at fetch and carry for the dippers, this week, while I think on you."

Blackie edged up and stood by Tom, so that the overlooker caught sight of her just before he turned away.

"And the lass can go and ask in the paintshop for work at lining, since she's got a touch for it."

Such sunshine swept across the clear side of Blackie's face! She jumped up and down, and hugged Tom, while Jonas' boy sniggered behind them, and Tom stiffened, and flinched back. But Blackie skipped across the yard, laughing, and danced through the paintshop door, and was gone.

So Tom went to learn to be a dippers' boy. Not that it was hard. He had to go to the opened kiln, and take up a basket of plates and dishes, filled for him from the kiln by two men working. They unstacked the piles of saggars—thick clay drums in which the ware had been put to bake—and filled up baskets. Tom carried the basket into the dipping shop, and handed the pieces, still warm from firing, to the dipper, who plunged them into a barrel of thick grey-white liquid, and then set them upon racks to drip a little.

At first Tom did well enough. He had only to walk, not run. True the basket was heavy, but then there was no plunging into the iron blast of heat from the furnace. A thin fine rain was falling, and he felt cool enough. Only as the morning wore on he felt cold rather than cool, and almost wished to slip into the drying-room oven, to warm up just for a moment before going on. And as he stood by the glaze barrel, handing plates, the smell of the glaze began to oppress him, and make his head spin. He was shivering as though from the running. He could hardly help himself, so long had he been running in these yards, from taking back an empty basket running—clattering up the steps that led to the kiln mouth.

"Eh, eh, slow and sober at this job, lad," said one of the men unloading saggars.

Each journey took Tom past the window where Blackie was working. He could hear the women's voices, chattering like birds on a bush. He heard the steady voice of the old man reading to them, and then the gossip again. He heard Blackie, her voice loud and piping, saying, "... and we'll have a house down by the river bank, and swept ... and little ones ..." and he missed his footing on the wet surface of the yard, and fell.

At first he did not realise that the crash smash and jingle sound was of his own making. It brought a press of workers to every door round the yard. It brought the overlooker out of his office, shouting. It brought Blackie's face up to the window behind Tom; and all the while broken fragments from Tom's basket were still rolling away, tinkling and skithering across the pavement.

"Up, you, and out!" said the overlooker. "Out of here, and don't you show your face here again!"

Still dazed, Tom got up. The overlooker turned on his heel.

"If you please, master, can I have my money?" said Tom.

"Your what?" said the overlooker.

"I've worked the best part of this week, master," said Tom, "and not been paid for it."

"And what think you is the worth of the ware you have just broken? Pay for that, and I'll pay your wages; but you'd do better far to take yourself off before I start counting the cost!"

Suddenly there was Blackie at Tom's side, putting her hand in his.

"And what are you doing here?" demanded the overlooker. "Back to your work, and sharpish!"

"If Tom goes, I go," said Blackie, in a small dry voice.

"Be it so then, foolish wifey," answered the overlooker. "Do you think I'll reckon o' that? World's full of wenches who can paint a line!"

"And I'll have my money afore I go," said Blackie, trembling. "I 'avent broken nothing."

The overlooker bestowed on her a terrible frown, but the workers were still lingering in the doorways. He put his hand in his pocket and gave her a shilling.

"Good riddance," he said.

Blackie and Tom walked forlornly through the gate, under the swinging bell, with Creep slipping along in the shadows behind them.

So up the incline, where the tub-boats rattled up and down, and the engines breathed noisily driving them, till the Pottery looked like nothing more than a cluster of dirty bottles smoking away down among the trees below.

Creep's boat beneath the willow looked rooted; the grass had grown into it from the bank, and the mooring rope was locked down to the ground by a criss-cross of couch grass laced over it.

"Do you think yon will move again?" said Tom, miserably.

"Gonna have to, in't it?" said Blackie.

"It will if I push it," said Creep.

12

Long after most of the boys had rushed out of the school, yelling; after the lanky, man-sized sixth-formers had dispersed, making meet-you-tomorrow arrangements with each other; when the football team had showered, changed, and gone home trailing their sports bags, and the Friday detention had been released in time to miss the bus, there was still a small solitary figure hanging about at the main gates. A bunch of teachers swept past, the Games master carrying the German assistant's case.

Looking out through the window, raising his eyes occasionally from his marking, the History master frowned briefly at the lingerer. His mind long attuned to mischief, he wondered what the wretch might be up to, and when he had marked the last essay on "Why was there no revolution in England comparable to the Revolution in France?", and annotated it *Shallow: do think for yourself* he took particularly long walking round, checking doors and windows, locking up every possible entry into the school.

When he emerged, locked the main door behind him, and set off across the gravel path between the lawns, the figure was still there.

He meditated accosting the boy and demanding what he was doing, then saw it was a younger boy, and recalling that he had locked everything up, and was already late, would have swept past had not the child stepped into his path, and said timidly, "Are you Mr Barker, please?"

"What do you want?" said Mr Barker, startled. He looked down at a shabby, almost scruffy child, very thin, with a pained and worried expression, and a touch of redness about nose and eyes that suggested hardship, or extreme cold, though the sun was shining. "You're not one of my boys," he said—a statement, not a question.

"No, sir," said the boy. "But one of your boys told me it was you what taught history in the posh school, and if you wouldn't mind very much, sir, could I ask you something?"

The History master looked at his watch. He had, in fact, just missed one bus, and had fifteen minutes to go before the next.

"Make it quick," he said.

"How do I find someone from the past?" said the boy.

Still more surprised, the History master paused. "Don't they teach history in your school?" he demanded.

"No, sir. Just topic work. On great explorers, and food in the past, and that."

Mr Barker put down his briefcase, and sat down on the low wall beside the gate. "Out of the mouths of babes ..." he said. Had he not always thought that new methods were frivolous, lacking framework, suitable only for the hopelessly stupid? And here was this (presumably stupid) child confirming.... Amazing when you think of some of the boys they *do* send here. Why am I not teaching this one? "So what exactly is it that you want to find?" he asked.

"Not some*thing*, sir. Some*one*. How do I look up someone from the past?"

"Well, it would depend what they're famous for. I'd try the *Dictionary of National Biography* first, for someone British. You'd find that in the Reference Room at the Public Library. That has just about everybody in it, who ever was anybody."

"But you mean special people, sir. Rich, and that. Inventors, and all."

"And all. Quite so."

"But what if someone was just poor and ordinary?"

"Ah, well, that's more difficult. Most people have always been born, laboured, and died without leaving any trace, without anyone noting them. Not many people could read and write till very recent times; few people paid for gravestones; millions of the poor were buried by the parish without any record except in a book. Parish records would be your best source. You'd just look for the name you wanted all through the birth, marriage and death columns of the parish register." Mr Barker was warming to his subject; his thesis had been on various anomalies in parish records of the seventeenth century. "How far back are you wanting to go?" he asked.

"Dunno," said the boy, looking alarmed and miserable at the same time. "Well, not before there was canals, I think."

"Late eighteenth," said Mr Barker. "Pity. Thousands of people moved into towns, or went to work in factories then, and it gets much harder to trace family names in parish documents. You can find out what life was like for the poor; that's relatively easy. Lots of books about that. There were Government commissions looking into working conditions, and recommending reforms, and they travelled the country talking to dozens of workers. These interviews are printed in their reports. All in the Parliamentary Papers. You'd learn a lot. Say, if the person you were looking for was a cotton-operative, you could find out exactly what it was like working in a cotton mill, at that time, but it would be a stroke of unbelievable luck if the very person you were looking for was one of those interviewed by the inspectors."

"Would that be impossible?" asked the boy.

"Well, it couldn't be *impossible*, could it?" said Mr Barker, talking more than half to himself. "After all, those interviewed must have descendants, living now, and so if one of those descendants went looking for them. ... Just exceedingly unlikely," he concluded.

"What papers did you say they would be in?" the boy asked.

"Parliamentary. All in the Public Library. Look, I don't want to encourage you on a wild goose chase...."

"The Library in Eden Street?"

"Oh, no. The main one, by the Butter Cross in the town centre. They have a big reference room there, and they keep all the stuff on local history, and all the P.P.s. Parliamentary Papers, I mean. Look, I'll write these things down for you, so you don't forget. It's a bit impressive, but don't be daunted. You've a right to read there." He handed the boy a sheet of paper torn from his diary with several titles, and the dates of some promising Parliamentary reports.

"Trying to trace your family, are you?" he said.

"Well, yes, sort of," said the boy, and the anxious tense face upturned to the History master actually seemed to threaten tears. Instead the boy coughed, and blew his nose into a dirty handkerchief. "Thanks a bomb!" he said, taking the paper.

The History master looked at his watch again, and sighed, and set himself to walk home, having missed yet another bus. He was feeling quite brisk and pleased with himself.

"Extraordinary who they send to us, and who they don't," he repeated to himself.

13

Even with Creep pushing, the boat was reluctant to move. It seemed to be stuck fast, and though Tom and Blackie both pushed, it would not budge. At last Tom cast a coil of rope across the cut onto the far bank, and then walking round by the nearest bridge, he pulled hard from the other bank, while Creep and Blackie pushed from the near one. Suddenly the boat swung free. It began to move rather fast, then, and Tom had to run, and jump aboard at the bridge hole.

Rapid it may have been, but it wasn't a smooth ride; a gloom lay heavily on them all, and they felt as if the boat itself were sullen, disliking this new journey.

"Oh, why did tha have to drop that basket, Tom?" Blackie wailed suddenly.

"Well, who asked thee to go an' bugger up thy job too?" he snapped. "Why din't tha keep tha silly mouth shut, and hang to what tha'd got? And if tha thinks I'm buttered up because you come away too, well I'm not!"

Creep slid up close beside Blackie, looking at her anxiously at this, but she just said, "Well, I'm with thee, aren't I?"

"It was Creep asked you along, not me," said Tom, sourly.

The boat didn't go far. It stopped in a mile or so, by a bridge taking a rutted cart track over the cut, between two fields, with nothing in sight but a flock of sheep, and a dew-pond in their pasture.

The children looked about, puzzled.

"Nowt's here," said Blackie.

"We could try pushing it again," said Creep.

But just then they heard the rumble of wheels, and a cart passed across the bridge. Looking up they saw it was piled high with coals.

"Ah," said Tom. "Come on, then. Let's spy out where that come from."

The track led up the hillside from the bridge a little way, to a clump of trees at the top. The three of them scrambled through the trees, and stood on the margin of the clump, looking down into a shallow valley. Some way off, just a step up the opposite rise, was a tall brick building, with an iron gantry built up alongside it, and a wheel, half within, and half without the building, slowly turning. Then there was a chimney, belching smoke, and beside that, on the ground, an enormous hemisphere of copper, shining and new. Beside the copper thing was a huge iron mechanism— two stout columns of green-painted metal, like tree trunks stood side by side, and atop them a vast arm tilted upwards. While they watched, it suddenly breathed loudly, and abruptly swung down to tilt the other way. As it swung, things slid and moved, and a wheel carrying chains spun round. There were several other little brick buildings standing by, and piles of coal, and horse carts coming and going, and men with barrows, and a line of women handling the coal in baskets, and taking out the larger lumps.

"What's that?" said Creep, when he had stared a good while.

"That's a mine," said Tom, slowly. "But it's a rummy one. There ain't no horse gin, there ain't no whimsy. There's just that great engine there. And I don't see what makes it go."

"It's a steam ginny, most like," said Blackie. "Like the one what worked the boats on the incline."

"I didn't know they could drive whimsy gear," said Tom. His voice was warm and thoughtful. "Think I'll just go on down there, and look around," he said.

"Tom ..." said Blackie. But she spoke to his rapidly receding back, as he strode away down the track. "Oh, well," she said to Creep, shrugging. "I ain't going to play tag-tail-along to anyone. Come'n let's scavenge."

She led him through the trees, to the edge of the little copse. There, where the trees kept the light of the sun off and a little spring made a marshy patch at the margin of the field, they found mushrooms growing. Blackie spread her threadbare skirt wide, and Creep picked and picked, and filled it with mushrooms. Then they wandered back to the track, and looked down towards the mine. They saw a bustle of coming and going there: a man in a dirty shirt loading a cart with a shovel; a man leading a pair of donkeys with panniers full of coal; but no sight of Tom. They sat a while; he did not come, and they took themselves off to the boat, where Blackie sat carefully sorting their gatherings, pinching and smelling each one in case it was a toadstool they had taken by mistake. Creep lay on the cabin roof, watching the upside-down world in the water, and glancing at Blackie, who just as often glanced up the hill.

When the sun began to slip down the sky, they set out once again to mount the slope, and sit on the edge of the wood, waiting for Tom.

"Do yer know what them birds are, Creep?" Blackie said, pointing to a crowd of birds that pecked at the field.

"No," said Creep. "I hadn't never seen a bird at all till the other day. You coulda told me they was fish what sing!"

Blackie chuckled.

"No, honest," he said.

"Must've been a funny place you come from," said Blackie. "Is that him?" She was looking towards the mine.

"Nope," said Creep.

"No, it in't," Blackie agreed. "I wish he'd come home. I'm getting cold."

"We could go on back ourselves," said Creep.

"All right," said Blackie. But she sat a while longer before she got up, and then went very slowly back.

They raked up the stove, and cooked the mushrooms. Blackie ate hers. It was slowly getting dark outside. At last they heard footfalls outside; the boat rocked briefly, and Tom appeared at the cabin door.

"Where 'ave you bin?" demanded Blackie.

"Getting me a job," said Tom. He looked very pleased with himself, but somehow uneasy. His mouth was set firm.

"Oh, Tom, you in't going down a mine!" cried Blackie.

"It's the trade I know; I got hardened to it, Blackie. It's all I'm good for, see."

"No it's not!" she said, fiercely. "I'll wager there in't anything you couldn't do, Tom-noddy!"

"You can drop a basket of coals, Blackie, without you have the world at your throat," he said.

Tears welled up in Blackie's eyes. She wiped them off with two angry strokes of the back of her hands. "It's 'orrible in mines, in't it?" she said. " 'Orrible and dangerous!"

"This mine's all right," said Tom, brightening. "Honest, Blackie. It's got a great steam engine pumping the water out so it won't get all squelchy; the engine's so strong it couldn't hardly flood, whatever happened. And they've got chains from the engine to wind up up and down the shaft, not like an old biddy winding up a rotten rope, like at t'other place. There won't be no ropes snapping and dropping poor bleeders down."

"Mines blow up, an' kill folk," said Blackie.

"This one won't," said Tom. "They've got a funny kind of lamps instead of candles; got a wire screen all round the light, and it don't make explosions. If it burn too bright, means fire-damp, and if it go out, means choke-damp; so either way you know to get out in good time. They've got canaries, too. Safe as home."

"Home don't fall down and crush you under it," said Blackie. "An' what's canaries for? Sing to you, or summat?"

"They put a pit-prop every yard," said Tom. "And the canaries are for if a bird falls off its perch you know that the air is bad, and out you get, quick."

"All right, then," said Blackie, head held suddenly high. "So it don't kill you. So you get all strong and stupid, thrutching coals. Thick body and thick head;

can lift an ox over a stile, and goes down to a chill like a babby. You be like that if you want!"

"Listen, it ain't that bad down there," he said, sitting down beside her. "They've got it fixed so you wouldn't believe it! All the way through the roads from coal face to pit shaft, they've got iron plates laid down, with the edges bent up a bit; an' the coal carts has little wheels that runs against the rims on the plates. They trolley along smooth and easy all the way, on them, Newcastle roads, they're called. The miners've even got a song about it."

"You're just coddling me, Tom," said Blackie.

"No, I'm not," said Tom. "Listen," and he raised a strong husky voice:

> *"God bless the man wi' peace and plenty*
> *That first invented iron plates!*
> *Draw out his life to five times twenty,*
> *And s-l-i-d-e him through the heavenly gates!"*

"Well," said Blackie at last. "I suppose. Only Creep'n me can't go down in the dark, can we?"

"No, well, I was trying to tell you, Blackie. ..."

"Eat your mushrooms," she said, suddenly giving him the bowl with the soggy black mess of mushrooms in the bottom.

"I've had me supper," he said. "Look, Blackie, I've fixed to go hurrying coals to a man called John Cautherly, who works down yon; and he's got a right bonny wife, and she's cutting down a jacket of hisn for me to put on me back, and there's a pair of shoes from a grown wench of hers that she'll have tipped for me feet; and there's a truckle bed in the kitchen for me....I just said I'd walk out a step and take leave of my friends, before I slept...."

When Blackie said nothing at all, he added, "There's

neither work, nor room for more than one. Goodbye, Blackie."

"Just goodbye, is it?" she said, suddenly angry. "And what am I to do?"

"You'll be all right, lass," he said, but he didn't look at her. He put his hands in his pockets, and looked at the drowned stars lying in the bottom of the cut. "You're tough."

She said nothing. "Tell you what," he said. "You can have Creep. I'll leave you our Creep to look after you. He can work, and he don't eat; he's a help and no bother, like a dog to a tramp."

"Well, he in't a dog, Tom-noddy, he's a person, and a person can't be give away, like an old coat!" she said.

"I don't know what he is," said Tom. "But he in't *real*; sometimes I can't hardly see him. He gets all fuzzy whenever we've a bite in our bellies. I can't hardly see him at all now."

"Well, in't that strange," she said, turning on him eyes welling with tears; tears that ran from her wide open eye, and her spoiled one, and coursed down both sides of her lop-sided face, "because he looks sharp and clear to *my* eyes, Tom; and clearer and kinder than you!"

"I never meant thee any harm, Blackie," said Tom, quietly. "And I wish thee good luck. But I must be going my road, now."

"Be it so, then," she said. "What's keepin thee? Did I ask thee to wait on?"

But when Tom was a minute or two away up the path, almost enveloped in the depths of evening, she suddenly called frantically after him, "Oh, Tom, be careful! Tom, mind the roof falling, and the foul air, Tom...."

A voice answered her from the deep darkness of the lane. "Don't fret!" it called. And then, "Creep! Dost tha hear me, Creep? I thank thee, little Knocker, for leading me out of harm's way!"

Blackie was still holding Tom's mushrooms. She held the bowl out to Creep, then when he shook his head, she dipped her fingers, and ate them herself, weeping into the bowl at the same time. Creep watched her silently.

"What shall us do, Creep?" she said, in a while.

"Go to sleep, maybe?" said Creep. He moved up close to her in the bracken bedding.

After she was sleeping soundly he heard the lapping of water on the boat, felt that softness of slight movement, like a touch of dizziness, and knew that the boat was moving again, unasked, through the night.

14

Christopher had never, as it happened, been to the Butter Cross in his life. He knew his way well enough around the streets of little terraced houses, all giving straight on to the pavements and backing up to houses in the street behind, which reached up and down and over the slopes of the part of the town where he lived. He knew his way to the shop on the corner, where he bought bubblegum and crisps and Vimto when he had money to spend. He knew his way through the council estate, across the great shadows of giant tower blocks, where his friends had addresses all of block and floor numbers, and there was a supermarket, and his school, made of glass and concrete, and a piece of grey plastic sculpture stood on an open area. The sculpture puzzled Christopher. It was called "The Worker" but it showed a man with a very small head and a convict haircut, who was so bulging about with enormous muscles that it looked as if he must have spent all his time on one of those body-building machines, and it was a mystery how he found time to do any work as well.

Buses for the town centre passed the statue, and

stopped at the school gate, but Christopher had no money; his pocket money had been stopped as a punishment for running away. Pauline had ten pence, but Christopher couldn't ask her. She was pretending all the time that she couldn't remember Creep, that there hadn't never been any Creep; and every time Christopher tried to remind her she only said "the Lady" had agreed with her.

So Christopher walked. He passed a lot of factories. They had dirt-blocked windows; the mud from the road when it was wet had smirched their blackened brickwork. They looked closed, abandoned, even though smoke from the chimneys showed that they were still in use. Between them, the road was lined with shabby shops, boarded up.

At last the road joined a wider one; there was a patch of land left over at the junction, just scruffy grass, criss-crossed with worn paths. The wider road had better shops, and tall buildings like flats, but identical blinds in all the windows. A Number 6 bus swept past Christopher, and down the road, showing him the way. Further along the wide road a few trees were planted, and the pavement got broader. A motorway crossed; the cars swept over and under, on raised concrete curves, surging and flowing in a continuous river of noise. Christopher, like others on foot, was led up and down a long way round on little foot bridges and through a subway, hundreds of steps. The other side of the motorway there was a huge hospital, and beyond that a road junction with signs saying *Town Centre. Butter Cross. Conveniences.*

Butter Cross turned out to be a street. A wide one, with huge clean department stores on either side, and a rather grand church made of soot-blackened stones, and a huge Town Hall built of stone blocks like madeira cakes, and covered with columns. Outside the Town Hall the road had been paved right across, and the cars and buses sent down a side street. On the pavement were wooden seats, concrete bowls planted with geraniums, and a lot of flagstaffs. There were more pigeons than people strutting there. But opposite the Town Hall was a huge building with pointed-arch windows, and a pointed arch door, all decorated with columns in black and purple marble, and rising to a row of crenelated turrets high above. And this building had a notice outside it that said *Central Library*.

Christopher climbed the long flight of steps and pushed his way through the revolving glass door. Inside, he found a marble-pillared hall in purple and green stones, a huge flight of curving white marble stairs, and a ceiling painted with undressed people floating around among some pink clouds and a lot of unwound bales of muslin. Christopher followed the signs marked *Reference*.

They led him into a huge book-lined room. Down the middle were rows of desks, topped with dark blue leather. A huge sign said SILENCE and a small one said *Enquiries*.

Christopher instinctively avoided *Enquiries*, and began to plod along the bays of shelves, reading the spines of books. *History of Technology*; *Debrett*; *Who's Who*; dozens upon dozens of books called *Hansard*. The Librarian caught up with him.

"Are you lost?" she asked. "The Children's Library is upstairs." One or two readers looked up, and stared.

"I don't want a children's book," said Christopher. "I want to look something up."

"You can look up lots of things in the Children's

Library. These books are all too difficult for you." She had dropped her voice to a whisper, but it still sounded very loud in the large silence, and someone reading near by was tutting at her.

"I want to find this," Christopher said, aloud, showing her the page from Mr Barker's diary.

She stared at it. Another librarian came up, a much older lady with blue-rinsed grey hair.

"Can he look at the Parliamentary Papers?" asked the younger one, looking doubtfully at Christopher.

"Third bay from the end, on the right," the older lady said crisply. "Are your hands clean?"

Christopher spread them out.

"All right. Now, mind. Don't make a noise and disturb people, or you'll have to leave. Understand?"

He nodded. "Keep an eye on him," the blue-rinsed lady said to her assistant.

Christopher went to the third bay from the end on the right. It was full of large volumes of even size, bound in heavy dark blue leather. He checked his note, and took down *1842, Vol XIV*, took it to a desk, opened its heavy cover, and began to read.

The book was hard to understand. It was reports from different parts of England. The reports were full of conversations, questions and answers given in full. But in a moment or two Christopher realised that the questions were being asked by some important sort of person, and answered by ordinary people, and that the book gave all their names, and told you what their jobs were, and how old they were. This is what the History master must have meant: the names were written in this book, and so if you were very lucky indeed you might find the person you wanted.

He began to read rapidly, barely stopping to notice

what was said. He was looking only at the names.

> "... Sarah Gooder, age eight, a trapper in the Gawber pit. 'Sometimes I sing, but not in the dark, I daren't sing then....' ... Ellison Jack, girl coal-bearer ... Margaret Leveston, six years old, coal-bearer ... Ann Ambler ... William Dyson.... James Taylor, alias Lump Lad, thrutches the waggons with his head and hands ... Tom Moorhouse, began to hurry coals for William Greenwood ... 'He struck a pick into my bottom ... I work now for John Cawtherly, and he finds me in victuals and drink.' ... Mary Davis, seven years old, keeper of an air-door ... William Withers, lost on Friday morning...."

Christopher read on. In a while he went and fetched from the shelves a volume marked *1843*. This volume had far fewer names in it. Instead it described workplaces.

> "The windows are very much broken, the shops are extremely close, crowded, and confined...."

or accidents:

> "They seldom lose a hand ... it only takes off a finger at the first or second joint ... sheer carelessness ... not looking about them ... sheer carelessness...."

The people in this volume were called

> "Witness No.96, A boy aged sixteen, as near as he can guess."

or just

> "Boy, aged twelve."

Christopher steadily turned the pages, scanning them swiftly for names. Whenever he looked up, the young woman from the *Enquiries* desk seemed to be looking at him.

"Jacob Ball,"

he read,

"12 years old, runner of dish moulds at Mr Rowley's earthenware factory … Sarah Griffiths, aged twelve, 'Please sir, all the family are very small.…' "

The print danced before Christopher's eyes. He read another page, letting his eyes slide over the words, searching out only names or children's ages. At last he got up, and sighed, and put the book away carefully in the gap among the ranked volumes. He looked along the shelf. So many!

On the way back along the Butter Cross, on his long walk home, he passed a little bridge parapet, between two shop-fronts, that he had not noticed on the way there. He scrambled up, gripping with the rubber toes of his plimsolls and his palms on the stone capping of the wall, to look over. There below was the canal, black and dank. It passed under the street; and some way off he could see it plunging directly under a huge new office block. The water was full of rubbish.

"It's as though people hate it," he said to himself. "As though they come for miles bringing their dirt specially to put in it. But it's nice, really. It goes to fields and woods and things."

He slid back down the pavement. "I haven't given up, Creep," he told the unseen water behind the wall. "It's just going to take a lot of time. But I'll read all them books if I have to. Honest."

A bus swept past him. He followed along its route, trudging home.

15

It was dark. There was no moon; only a thin pale band of sky right down low, against which the outlines of chimneys showed; chimneys on a row of narrow houses. The boat had stopped. Creep came out of the cabin and stood on the deck. He couldn't understand what had woken him, for there was no sound in the muffled night, but the boat had lodged itself against the towpath, and perhaps that had jogged him.

As he stood looking, a window a little way off on the other side of the cut was suddenly brightly lit, the window frame making a black grid on the yellow rectangle, with the top edge slightly arched. And beside it another window frame was faintly appearing, and another even fainter beside that, and a mere grey ghost one last in line. Then the second window brightened to full shine, and the faint gleam travelled further, and filled in more pale windows, and as one after another the lights were lit within, more and more windows appeared in the line, and brightened, and then blazed out fully lit, all along a long, long row.

"That's a big place; that's enormous," murmured Creep to himself. For the seepage of light from one window to another told him that it was all one large room where the lights were being lit. And as he murmured, suddenly, at the far end of the long row of windows, a new one flashed into view, above the row, and the light began to flow back towards him, window after window, along a second floor. And when the last window in the second row was bright, a third row began, and the stacks of yellow oblongs jumped the band of darkness where the wharf extended, and began to shine doubled in the water below. A fourth and fifth row were shining when Blackie came suddenly from sleep, and stood beside Creep, watching. The lights climbed on, row above row, as though mounting to the sky; and at last, as an eighth row began, Creep could see, above that, the black outline of the building itself, just faintly visible, looming up against a dimly brightening sky. They could see a chimney, too, standing up immensely tall against the sky, and the shadowy smoke passing across the grey early dawn.

"In't it big, Creep?" said Blackie, in a whisper.

And as she spoke they both became aware of sounds, and lowered their eyes from the sky. Along the canal bank people were moving. They were coming slowly, and silently, in great numbers, crossing a bridge, going all towards a lamp, just now lit, that showed to Creep and Blackie a gate into the vast windowed place. The crowd seemed to be sleep-walking, so silent were they, and so dream-like and sluggish their pace. And some of them were little children. Little children trailing along behind larger ones, led by the hand by young women in shawls and clogs, or carried bodily in the arms of men. They came like moths out of the dark, and crossed through the pool of light at the mill door;

and Creep saw one child, arms across the shoulders of two others, making walking movements with his feet, though his feet did not touch the ground for he was supported by his friends.

"Don't let's stop here, Blackie," said Creep. "Let's ask the boat to go along some more."

"We better not, Creep," she said. "Whatever that is, it's work for scraps like us. Well, like me. And there in't all that much work in the world; and work's better than hunger, by far. You in't ever hungry, so you don't know. We'll wait and see, when they come out, if we can ask among them for a place for me."

They waited. The day came up, cool and grey. The mill was vast, of strident red brick, with bands of yellow between the rows of windows. Across the top it said TRIUMPHANT in yellow brick letters. Blackie sat on the boat and watched; Creep went exploring. The mill stood in fields, but as he walked back a step the way the boat had brought them in the dark, he came to a place where the canal crossed on a stone bridge above the streets of a town, and he could look down on lines of houses, small and grey, with slate roofs and smoky chimneys, from which the people in the mill must have come. Creep saw that there was a market going on in one of the streets below, and he climbed down the steep bank at one end of the aqueduct, and stole an apple for Blackie.

"It makes a noise, that place, all the time," said Blackie, when he got back to her. It did indeed rumble continuously, but as though to disprove her, as she spoke, it stopped. A few people came out of the gates and sat on the grass outside, or along the canal bank, to eat.

"I could go and ask them now," said Blackie. She

stopped to push her fingers through her tousled hair, and straightened her ragged coarse pinafore, using the canal water as a looking glass. But she had hardly gone a step or two, not even reached the bridge that crossed to the mill wharf, when the great rumbling started up again, and the people melted away, picking up their bags and hastening within. Blackie came back again, kicking her toes in the dust to wait once more.

The dusk crept up slowly, and the two waiting children watched the windows lit up again row upon row. And they had long been lit, and the moon was rising behind the topmost windows and lighting the floating movement of the chimney smoke into the sky, before at last the rumbling sound ceased again, and the people began to walk home, leaving behind them the lights going out one by one, and the glow seeping away from one window after another.

Like moths they came, silent, heads bowed. They stumbled and staggered, and the children among them were pulled along, eyes closed, or some few carried away sleeping. Blackie jumped up and ran off, threading her way among them, asking questions. Creep followed to the bridge, and there stood staring, his face set still and gloomy. And the throng of folk passed under the lamplit arch of the gate, Creep saw they were moth-like in more than their dark movements; a pale soft downiness adhered to their hair and clothes; he shuddered at it without knowing why, as at the furriness of a moth's night-wings. He could hear Blackie's fluting voice, and the flat weary tones of answers; by and by she came back to him and said there was a man who had bid her come again in the morning and he would see. She seemed content enough with that.

The man was called Mr Dean. He stood in a little office just within the gate. He nodded at Blackie, and stared pointedly at her spoilt face.

"You have worked before, I see," he said.

"Yes, master."

"Well, well, we prefer a child who is accustomed to work. I will see if any of the workers has a place for you. Come by me, now."

Blackie followed him; and Creep followed her. Mr Dean swung back a door, and with Creep stepping close behind her, Blackie entered an ocean of roaring noise that struck so hard it felt as though it would have swept them away, as on a flood of water. The moment after the noise, they felt the warmth of the place. It was as hot as the hottest summer day, and as damp as the wettest one, and it smelt; it smelt, Creep remembered, like the washing on the rack before the fire in a small kitchen from somewhere long ago, when the wet from the clothes had run down the fogged window-panes, and the sheets had been scorched from being too near the stove. They had walked not a yard or two along the line of great black barrel-like machines standing in rows all down the huge room, before there was a soft tickle on Creep's face; something fine resting there, as though he had walked through cobwebs, and the tickle and cling at the back of his throat and in his nostrils made him cough. But the noise swept his cough away, so that he did not hear it himself. Blackie, too, felt it, for he saw her brush her cheek with the back of her hand, saw her too cough, unheard.

Mr Dean walked down the long room, shouting in the noise, talking to the women working there; Creep watched. The great machines were being fed with soft white wadding; huge drums covered with wire teeth combed it out fine, and it fell in a lacy thin sheet, like cobweb indeed, from the front of the machines, where little girls were gathering it up with two hands, and feeding it in a long soft coil into tall drums.

They were led the length of this floor, and out through a door at the far end. "Nowt for thee in the carding room," said Mr Dean, mounting some stairs. "We'll try the drawing flat."

He swung open another door. Once more the unmuffled noise engulfed them. Swimming in the sound, and the close air, Blackie and Creep walked behind him. The room was full of machinery, stretching down the whole length of the mill, and right across the wide room. Spinning axles and wheels ran along the ceiling, turning wheels from which bands looped and crossed, driving the machines. The soft coils of cotton from the cans filled on the floor below was being drawn between hundreds of rollers, the first turning slowly, and the next faster, and the next faster yet, so that it was pulled out straight and fine, before it was taken up by more pairs of hands, lightly twisted, and coiled down into drums again. Children came and went, barefoot, running, changing full drums for empty ones. Men and women strode along the corridors between the lines of machines, putting together the strips of cotton when they broke. And all was warm, and moist, and drowned in noise. As they passed, an overlooker turned a handle and let a gust of steam into the room, and then spoke to Mr Dean. Creep could not hear his words, but he knew well enough what a shake of the head means.

So Mr Dean led them higher yet, and brought them into the spinning rooms. And here the machines were topped with four racks of spindles, all spinning round at once, from end to end of the great room. The threads from the spindles stretched to other spindles mounted on a frame towards the floor level, and this frame was on wheels, as they watched it swept forwards, away from the machine across the floor, and threads were drawn out and twisted rapidly, and then it paused, and swept back again, and the finished thread was drawn up on to bobbins on the machines. Under the web of threads little children crawled, sweeping up the cotton waste, and the flyings that filled the air and snowed down in fine dust upon the floor, going upon hands and knees, and keeping out of the way of the machinery as best they could. And up and down the length of each machine went workers, a grown man or woman, and two little children to mind each one, who were twisting together the ends of thread whenever they broke.

Still in Mr Dean's wake they moved past one machine after another. Small children were watching the spindles near the floor; when a thread broke they stopped the movement of the offending spindle with a raised knee jammed against it, and bent over the ends, left and right hand, twisting them together. The grown workers moved hastily along the rows, removing the full bobbins, and putting empty ones in their place. And among them was a neat, pallid young woman, with a tired smile, who needed a "piecener" and took Blackie on.

Creep slipped aside and sat on the window ledge, watching the whirling ranks of bobbins with the white thread snowballing on to them, which stretched as far as he could see.

"My name is Ann Abbot," the woman was telling Blackie, voice raised above the rattle and hum, and the bird-like chirping of the turning spindles. "Thou'lt work for me, and I'm to pay thee." She showed Blackie how to piece the ends together. Then she got from her apron pocket an apple, and said, "Now if when I come looking, there are no ends hanging down all along this row, the apple is thine, dearie, but if the ends are all hanging down and the spindles stopped, I'll be constrained to chide thee."

Creep got down from his perch, and slipped along the line of spindles. He watched Blackie, knee raised, head bent, in just the moment when the sweep of the frame paused before receding, twist the first loose end together, and start the spindle going again, and then he skipped to the other end of the row, and began to watch for ends to mend himself.

It seemed at first all was well enough. True the air in the room was full of cotton flyings, and made one's throat tickle, and one's lungs feel creaky. But it was light and clean, and twisting two ends of thread together is light work compared to forging chain links. But the machine worked so fast, and the ends broke so often, that however fast Blackie worked along the spindles there was always one slowing and stopping with its end down behind her as well as in front. Ann Abbot may have offered an apple to keep Blackie working hard; but there was also an overlooker, who had a whip in his belt, and who came up and down, looking hard at what was about.

When it came to dinner time, and the machine stopped; the quiet flowed slowly back around them and slowly stilled the ghosts of banging and humming in their ears that the noise left behind it. The workers withdrew to the ends of the room and sat down to eat, and there were many little children coming out from behind the machines, whose walk was all knock-kneed, and many of these saw Creep clear enough.

"He helps me," said Blackie. Now they sat and talked together, the grown women seemed all rather pale, and more than one coughed into a handkerchief, and left blood there.

The dinner time was not long. In the afternoon, as it drew into evening, the children became sleepy, and Creep saw the spinners cuffing them to keep them awake. Long before the end of the day, when the lamps had been burning, for hours already, and the smell of oil came with the cotton fluff to sicken them, Blackie was half asleep, sleep-walking up and down; Creep was nodding, and missing half the threads at his end, so that Ann came and scolded Blackie.

When at last the huge engine came to rest, and the vast roar of noise was stilled, the little boy who pieced at the next machine, was still, eyes closed, making the twisting movements with his fingers, though the spindles had all drawn back, and there was no more thread there. Then his spinner came and shook him awake, and he stumbled off unsteadily home.

"I'll give thee wages a penny a day this week, to help thee buy dinners," Ann told Blackie. "And thou must be here by six in the morning. Divent be tardy, mind, for if thou art, the overlooker will beat thee, and I can't keep thee from it."

It was only a short step to the boat, just through the mill yard, and over the bridge, and along the bank; even so Blackie sat down to rest twice on the way back, and was asleep as soon as she sat; and the second time Creep picked her up, and carried her, with difficulty, for thin and small as she was, he was himself thinner, and little bigger. And so they got home.

They were not late on the morrow, and Blackie was not beaten; other children were. It was common enough, if they slackened for a moment, or as they became tired. They cried and wept, but none could hear them, for the noise swept the sound away like the fall of a pebble in the roar of a mill-race. Common though it was for a child to get beaten, William Kershaw fared worst of all. He made his master angry beyond the common run, and brought the whole flat to a close. He worked right next to Creep and Blackie, but the first they knew of it was that the machines suddenly stopped, and in the gap where the noise had been there came instead the sound of someone shouting curses. Everyone gathered to look. William had got his sleeve caught up in the drive-band of his machine, and was in peril of being dragged into the rollers bodily. Someone had unhitched the belt that drove all the machines on that level, and he was safe, white and trembling. Two men struggled to turn the wheels the wrong way, and so free him, for he was held by his clothes. The overlooker arrived to see what had stopped the work.

"I'll leave him to you," the overlooker said to William's master, when he was finally got out, and set upon his feet again. The spinner took William up bodily, and set him in an empty skip. Then he took down the billy-roller, which runs along the top of the machine, and began to beat the boy. The machines started up again, and wiped out his screams, so that Blackie, with tears in her eyes, could see his stretched mouth, and his screwed-up eyes, but could not hear him.

At dinner time William was leaning in a corner by the stairs, being sick, and bringing up blood with the vomit. Blackie gave him a sip of milk from her pannikin, and spoke kindly to him.

"Stop whinging, thou good for nowt!" said his master. "Thou canst not work at all; thou dost all ill. This wench has been here a week only, and mends her ends faster than thou dost!"

"Tha's not fair!" wailed William. "She has a helper. Comparing two hands to one is not fair!" and he began to be sick again.

'Thou hast belted all the wits out of him, James," said another spinner. "Thou hast too heavy a hand."

"Why doesn't he run away?" Creep asked Blackie that night.

She sighed. "We've been about the world enough to know there's not so many places to run to," she said. "Better or worse, there's no knowing which. Or even back round to the same like Tom. Happen he'll be too ill to work tomorrow."

But William came the next day. The engine was late starting, for the mill-owner was showing a gentleman round the works, and wished to do so in quiet.

The gentleman was rosy and round-faced. He wore a soft velvet jacket, and a frilled shirt, and fine black trousers and a tall round hat. A gold watch hung at his front. He looked round the machines, and never met the eyes of the silent workers, standing barefoot, at their frames, waiting for him to go.

"You have a very ill-looking set of people working for you," he said in a loud voice. "They look miserable and thin."

"They've eaten all the nettles for ten miles around," said the owner sourly, "and now they've no greens to their soup."

"Shocking, shocking!" said the visitor. "Do you mean to tell me, sir, that you pay them not enough for their food?"

"Don't care for them," said the owner. "Why should you care for them? How can I sell you goods cheap, if I care for them?" And he showed the visitor out.

And just then, when the grand folk had left, and the machines were all standing still and idle for a moment longer, there was shouting, a woman's voice raised in anger.

"Oh, don't, Mother. Oh don't fuss! It'll be but the worse for me!" cried William's voice, from across the frames.

"You wretch! You ugly brute!" William's mother was yelling at his master. "Let you just look at my boy's back! That's not done just to keep a lad awake, I'll warrant! There's some on you takes pleasure beating little lads, God forgive you! God may forgive you, but nivver will I! Do you think because the owner doesn't mind it, you may do anything? There's magistrates in this town, and they can be gone to if poor folk is hard pressed enough; you mind what I say!"

And all around, behind the lines of bobbins, the workers glanced at each other, and smiled grimly.

"That's right, missus—you tell'un!" called someone down the room. But then the drive-bands began to turn, and the bobbins and spindles to dance, and the noise to rise over them all, and the work began.

William's mother marched out. But she had no sooner gone than William was put in the skip again, and the billy-roller was off, and his master was beating him again, for telling.

"Where will she have went?" cried Ann, screaming to be heard by the spinner next to her.

"To the engine-feeder's house, I shouldn't wonder," the other replied. "He is kin of hers." And to his piecener he said, "Run, Dick, fetch her back here."

Dick ran. And so in a little while William's mother came back. And the engineer on the flat turned a wheel or two, and brought all the machines on their level to rest, all the drive-bands running free; and the spinners and pieceners all drifted silent on their bare feet, coming through the lines of frames till they could see. But Ann stood fast, and Blackie with her, since they could see from where they stood. Creep edged up beside Blackie, taking the chance to mend a broken thread while all was still.

"What was you beat with?" William's mother asked him.

"Go home, Ma, thou makest it worse," he said, hoarsely, the tears still wet on his cheeks.

"It was the billy-roller, missus," said the engineer, quietly.

And with that she seized the billy-roller, and struck William's master with it, hard over the head, and then again across the shoulder, and then again on the other. He staggered away from her, putting up his arms to fend her off, and she cracked him on the elbow, so that he yelled loudly, and backed away, and she marched after him, wielding her heavy weapon, and crying, "Bully! Wretch!" at the top of her voice.

And as they came down towards Creep, he looked up and laughed.

His laugh rang out, high-pitched and clear. Blackie looked round as though she had never heard the sound before, and at once a great wave of laughter swept through the room, as everyone, large and small, laughed too. They laughed, and nudged each other, and called rude names, and chuckled, and when at last the gales of mirth died down, William's mother put the roller back, dusted her hands together, and marched out to catcalls and cries of "Huzzah!"

Creep was still standing at the end of Blackie's frame, in the midst of the press of workers, with a loose end of cotton in his hand.

"Why, who is this?" said Ann, in astonishment. And Creep saw that everyone was looking at him, looking at him and seeing him plain. He stood dumb and terrified.

"Where didst tha spring from?" said another worker.

"He's been here all the time," said William.

"Don't talk daft, lad," said the engineer. "We've never had sight of him before."

Blackie ran to Creep, and put her arm round his shoulder. And Creep suddenly wailed aloud, with his two hands pressed to his belly, "Oh, Blackie, I'm so *hungry*! I'm clemmed to death!"

16

The large blue volumes of Parliamentary Papers lay round Christopher on the reading room desk. Many pages seemed to be tables, figures, lists of workers. There were even blank copies of printed forms that had been sent round for people to fill in. But there were also names, voices. Christopher was getting good at scanning, letting his eye run over pages at a time, hardly stopping.

> "... Charles Burns, Peter Benet, James Smart, overlooker .."

only now and then his attention caught on something, and he found himself reading more than the bare name, hearing the voice on the page:

> "Joseph Badder, spinner: 'I have frequently had complaints against myself by the parents of children for beating them. I used to beat them. I am sure no man can do without it who works long hours. I told them I was very sorry after I had done it ...'"

"Is that child here *again*?" murmured one librarian to the other, frowning across the room.

"Been here since first thing. Not doing any harm."

"But how *peculiar*! Whatever is he *doing*?"

"He's reading the P.P.s. And a child who is capable of reading the P.P.s for weeks at a time is perfectly capable of complaining to an M.P. if we turf him out, I'd say."

"Well, of course I wasn't thinking of turfing him out; I'm just curious, that's all."

"Child prodigy?"

"Hardly. Try talking to him. He doesn't make any kind of sense; he doesn't really seem to know what he is doing."

"I suppose he'll go when he's read the lot!"

So Christopher read on. The air of the reading room smelt slightly dusty, slightly leathery. The sun fell into it through high windows, but before it reached the desks had lost its open-air exuberance, and become bookish, stiff and geometrical. Other readers came and went. As Christopher became tired, he fell back into the habit of slowly and carefully reading through, instead of just skimming. The work got slower.

> "Could you calculate how many miles you had to run a day when piecing?—At coarse work I had heard it say (sic) that they have to walk from thirty to forty miles a day and do their work; but fine factories is not so severe. When you were in a coarse mill, for how many successive hours had you to work?—I worked in summer time from five in the morning to a little after twelve; and then the mill would start a little before one, which left threequarters of an hour's rest, which ought to be a full hour. That leaves a quarter of an hour of which the children are robbed to enrich the mill owner

137

Then in the seven successive hours you worked, you either walked, or ran; how much?—That would be the better half, I believe. I would have to go near twenty miles.

Without sitting during that time?—Without sitting down at all.

And you said that in the beginning of the day was one of the times when you were most fatigued?—Yes, by the legs being stiff; but after the middle part of the day the more the hours increased the more the pain increased in the knees ..."

Christopher realised suddenly that he had read half a page of Thomas Wilson. He wrenched his mind away, turned the page, and saw:

"NATHANIEL CREEP Sworn and examined by Mr Cowell, 28th June, 1833."

A hot prickly tremor ran down his spine as he read on.

"Witness does not know the date or place of his birth; was an orphan. Has worked at sundry different occupations. Has seen coal hurrying, chain link making, mould running in a pottery, and piecing cotton before he went to navvying. Crippled on a barrow run. (Witness cannot stand straight, and can go only with two sticks) Married. Four children living.

Will you give us your opinion of the severity of labour in cotton mills?—It is hard, but there are other trades worse.

What is worse, in your view?—Chain and nail making.

Why is that?—Well, the hours worked can be as long as those in a factory. Then there is no knowing what may be done to children when they work in twos and threes under the direction of a master who has none to o'erlook him, and may do as he pleases. Then there is the nature of forge work, at which accidents are common.

In the course of your experience, would you say that children are anywhere worse used than in cotton mills?—They are nowhere so often beaten, I think.

Why is that, in your view?—The workers cannot do their work if the children do not do theirs; and the hours are so long that the children must be beaten to keep them awake.

Why do not the parents take their children away, if they find them ill-used?—They cannot afford to. Sometimes the children work for their own father and mother, and it is that father or mother who beats them, to keep them from falling, sleeping, into the machinery. But there are many parish apprentices among the child workers, and others who have no parent to care for them. They are in desperate plight, having no friends in the world but each other.

Was that your case, when you were a boy?—It was. I have had a paper printed, giving the story of my life and hardships. I will bring it to you, if you so desire. (The witness brought me the next day a broadsheet, entitled THESE ARE SOME NOTES OF MY LIFE, NATHANIEL CREEP. WRITTIN BY HIM. Enclosed for the attention of the Central Board.)"

Christopher turned the page. There was no more about Nathaniel Creep, only the deposition of Thomas Yates. He began to search frantically through the volume, looking for the rest. Then at last he sat, staring at the page. Perhaps it wasn't him ... this person sounded just like all the others; and *he* wasn't Nathaniel ... perhaps ...

"Witness cannot stand straight ..."

he read, over and over again.

17

Blackie said, "We shall be paid today, Creep, love, and I'll buy thee thy supper."

"Get that beggar out of here!" said the overlooker. "And you, Ann's wench, whatever you be called, if you go bringing the rabble in here with you, you'll work here no longer!"

And so as the spindles began all to turn again, and the noise rose round them like the waters of an ocean, Creep made his way down again, and out into the open air. At the foot of the stairs he passed by the engine house, its great doors opened wide to admit fresh air to the seething room where men stripped to the waist shovelled coal into the boiler. Looking in, Creep stared at the great fly-wheel, as high as three floors of the mill, spinning smoothly round, and the massive bands going up from it through a slot in the building to wheels for each floor above, and he saw the shining slide and thrust of the pistons that drove it all. A gust of air came out at him, smelling wet and scorched. Creep passed by.

Outside the mill were streets, with people walking about and looking at Creep as he passed. He flinched from their sharp, focused glances, knowing they were seeing him, and terrified of them. He passed a stall at a street corner, and dared not steal an apple, though he grew more famished with every step.

At last he retreated back to the boat, and hid away in it. By and by he came out, and took a handful of the green plants growing by the towpath, and ate them; but he spat them out as soon as he began to chew, his tongue curling in his mouth with the bitter dryness they left upon it. He put a stone in his mouth, and sucked it. He could find no rest. When he walked up and down the canal bank, he found himself so weak after a step or two that his legs doubled under him, and he staggered to the deck of his boat, and sat down upon it; but when he sat there the cramps in his belly, and the yearning in his mind for food fidgetted him, so that in a moment or two he got up again, and paced about. The day crept by, stretching each moment.

In the afternoon he was slumped on the boat, leaning up against the cabin side and gazing with glazed eyes and drooped lids at the gloomy prospect of the mill, looming up between him and the sun. "Oh, Chris," he said softly. "Oh, Chris, I wish you could find me. I shouldn't of run away...."

He was sitting there still, drowsing in troubled sleep in the darkness, when Blackie came from the mill. She had brought a bag of oatmeal and a pennyworth of treacle, and she mixed them into a cold gruel, and woke him with a bowl in her hand.

He ate it wolfishly, cramming it into his mouth, wiping and scraping with his fingers, licking them clean. Blackie sat watching him, in the light of a candle she had lit in the cabin, which spilled a little way onto the deck outside.

"Could you do with more, Creep?" she asked.

His face answered her, and his swiftly offered empty dish. She filled it again for him, and again watched him devour it.

"You've gone different, you have," she said.

"Where's your porridge, Blackie?" he asked her.

"I'm not hungry," she said, quickly. He looked, stricken, at his bowl, but it was already empty.

"You shouldn't have done that, Blackie," he said. "You'll be sorry for it before tomorrow."

"Happen I shall," she said, smiling her lop-sided smile. "What we going to do, Creep?"

He stood up. He looked down the reach of dark water, in the depths of which the moon swam, and his own reflection showed sharp and black in the still water. "I shall have to find work," he said. "You can't feed two."

"There might be work here, Creep," she said shakily. "Somewhere right near ... and good safe work ... and good money ... and we'll make the boat real cosy ... and have pots and pans to the fire, and blankets to the bunk...." Her voice died away. "You mightn't have to go far," she said, almost in a whisper

"Perhaps not," he said, dully.

In the morning he stirred first. He rose, and looked around. He found some milk Blackie had brought, and lit a few sticks in the stove, and put it to warm before he woke her. Then he filled his own bowl with water, and put just enough milk in to cloud it, to look as if he had some too. Then he woke her, and they sat by the small warmth of the stove, and drank.

"Shall we go our road?" she asked him. "I could go along with thee."

"Best not, Blackie. That Ann thou workest for is kind enough. From bad to worse is the way I'm going."

"Then I must walk. I don't care to be late."

"I'll go with thee, that far," he said, getting up, and giving her his hand.

At the mill gate she turned to him, and said, her face bright, "I hope thou findest something, near by; and I shall come tonight and find the boat still there, and we shall sup together ..." Her words trailed away.

"You'll be all right, Blackie," he said. "You're tough, love. Fare thee well, now."

"Oh, Creep!" she cried, as he turned away. "Oh, Creep, I'm *glad* you're real! I am that glad!" And then she was away among the others, going in through the dark gateway.

Creep untied his boat, and sat upon it, but it did not go. He talked to it, speaking of work, of seeking a place. ... It did not move. By and by he took the rope across his shoulder and hauled it along. He heaved it past the mill, where a whiff of the oil and cotton smell was born across the cut to him, making him pause a moment with a picture of Blackie in his mind's eye making a spasm at his heart. Then he went on. He didn't go fast, with only his own strength to take him. He was looking for another town, another kind of work.

He had gone a long way, several days without finding either, when he came instead to a line of low hills, rising gently from the fields and coverts round him, like a line of soft green sleeping waves. The canal went towards them, and then suddenly stopped. It just came to an end, going up to a green bank in the midst of nowhere. Creep tied up the boat, and walked on a bit, puzzled.

Just beyond the green bank that barred his way, the cut continued, but continued as an open gash in the land, empty of water. And following round the curve of the dry channel, Creep came suddenly upon a cutting in the making, with gangs of men working in a great wound in the hillside, labouring to dig a way forward into the side of the hill. In a sea of mud, muddied themselves from head to foot, they were struggling to bring barrow-loads of dirt away, hauling it up the slopes of the excavation to dump it at the top. Creep watched the work, wandering among men and horses. Lines of planks were laid steeply up the banks of the cutting; a pulley was set at the top of each, with a rope round it; a boy led a struggling horse down the slope, pulling on this rope, while the other end was tied to a barrow which an agile man steered upwards, fighting to keep its wheel running on the steep line of planks. Below the barrow-runs a clangour and the sounds of shouting rose from where the heart of the hill was being picked and shovelled, and loaded into the barrows.

A little way off the cutting was a huddle of squalid huts. Creep made his way in that direction.

"What's doing here?" he asked a tough ragged man in heavy boots, who was sitting at the door of a little bothy made of turf and roofed with straw. A line of these dens, several deep, straggled away across the field.

The man answered in a voice of strange colour, that Creep could barely follow. "Whoi, it's the great canal cutting; cutting, tunnel, then tunnel again, to get across the hill, see."

"The canal that stops back yonder?"

"That's her. Can't go no further now; but when us brave boys have done, yull go ter the north, plain, river and sea. When us gets through this wicked hill."

"Who's the ganger here?" asked Creep, thinking about this.

"The contractor? That's he, on a brown pony, coming along down thereabouts."

Creep followed the man thus pointed out to him, and when he came up to him, looked at a hard, wide-browed brown face, and said, "Canst thou find work for me, master? Or I'll starve."

The man frowned down at Creep. "You don't look up to much," he observed. "Right peaky, you look. What do you think you could do?"

"I can do what others can, I reckon," said Creep. "I can do what I must."

The man nodded at that. "I'll put you on a barrow-run," he said. "The money's very fair; very good. But God help you if you slip. I'll give you a tommy-note to get boots from the company store. You'll work a good while to redeem it. And if that's not good enough, good day to you."

"I thank you, master," said Creep. And following directions, he made his way towards the workings, passing through the press of men working at the bank edge and going among them till he was lost to view, becoming one among the others.

18

Christopher picked up the volume, and began to carry it to the enquiry desk. He knew exactly which of the two behind the desk he wanted to speak to; the one who worried about him less, the one with blue-rinsed white hair, and a cool expression. He measured his progress past the long line of bookcases, slowing up when she turned away, and presenting himself at just the right moment.

"I would like to read this," he said, showing her,

> THESE ARE SOME NOTES OF MY LIFE,
> NATHANIEL CREEP

in the book he held. "And it doesn't seem to be part of this book."

"No," she said, looking, "and I rather doubt if we'd have something as obscure as that. Unless ... unless it happened to be somebody local; we do have some nineteenth century pamphlets of local interest. There's a separate catalogue of them over there. Do you know how to use a catalogue?"

He shook his head.

"Come, and I'll show you. There, don't look so

worried. See: all the titles are on these cards, listed in alphabetical order, going by the author's name. So we want C." Her fingers shuffled the cards deftly, "Carstairs, Craven,—Ronald, Craven,—William…" she muttered. "Creel, Creely, Creep—yes! Look; you're in luck; we've got it." She sounded as pleased as if she had wanted it herself. Christopher stared at the card.

"Where?" he said.

"In the stacks. Where we keep the reserve collection. Go and sit down and wait. Can you wait? And I'll bring it to you."

It was a slim red leather volume. Inside, the pages were all yellow, and ragged at the edges all round. The lines of print were not quite even, the letters not all straight. It looked old, and it smelt strongly of dust. Christopher turned the flyleaf, feeling slightly sick.

NATHANIEL CREEP: WRITTIN BY HIM

he read.

> "I am a chance child. As to what town or parish I
> was born in, of that I have no recollection at all,
> for my mother took against me, I suppose for that
> my father had used her ill, and kept me for the
> most part locked in a cupboard, though she did
> what she could for my half-brother and sister. My
> brother it was that fed me, for my mother
> minded not if I starved or no…."

"Oh, Creep!" cried Christopher, with the tears welling up in his eyes. "It *is* you! I've found you!"

A voice said, "Had you better stop reading that, son, if it's upsetting you?" The librarian was leaning over him.

Desperately he clutched the book to his sweater.

"No!" he said. "No, I'm all right. I've got to know

what happened, see? I can't sleep for worrying what happened to him!"

She looked puzzled. "Well, if you're sure you're all right. But please handle that book carefully; it's very old."

Christopher laid it down flat again, smoothed the page, wiped his eyes surreptitiously with the back of his hand, and read on:

> "It happened they were knocking down the row of houses in which my family lived, and when they came to the house next ours they made a hole in the wall in the side of the nook below the stair wherein I was confined, and so I got out by that, and made my way about, looking for work. I put my hand to several things but they never come to much. I worked for a while in a cotton mill, but I got turned off from there, and at that there was nothing for me but to go navvying. Building canals was very rife at that time. First I led the horse on the barrow-runs; then when I had my strength on me (I had been sickly when a child) I dug and shovelled, and ran the barrows with the rest of them. I was proud of my strength till the day that I fell beneath a barrow and had my hip and my back broken. They got a doctor to me after three days, but he could do nothing for me. The other men put a hat round for me, and got up a guinea to support me. From the day of this accident I have needed a crutch and stick, but I thank my God for it, for it laid me in bed for thirteen week, and while I was lay up I began to feel very strongly the desires to learn to read. A young man I know came to read to me, and to show me my letters, and when I could get up I went to night school, and to the Primitive Methodist Sunday school, and what little I had

learned pleased me very greatly, and I got mixed up with the Primitive Methodists, which I have been from that time. Then Thos Cooper gave me The Rights of Man of Thos Paine to read, and I found my feeling much got up by that, and I joined with Thos Cooper and others in a sect called the Chartists, and so got to be Seccy of the local club. There was meetings near every night, and over 30,000 at one gathering at the Wrekin. Then when some of my friends were imprisoned, and I had to take more care what society I was mixed up in, a man called James Alford, made a friend of me, and put me in his shop to learn being a printer. Sometimes he printed matter which might have sent us all to prison or transported, but even though I went to the Methodist Chapel then instead of to meetings, I spoke nothing about it, for I would not for my life have done those men any harm. In those days I had a fancy, very troublesome in my mind, that I was lost, and someone was looking for me. I had felt so from a boy, but when I was working first for James Alford, then seeing how great a part in life for other folks was played by their kin, I could not stop from wondering about my own. At last I took a day off from the printing works, and walked back along the canal as far as I could remember having come as a boy, and there I put a writing upon a bridge. I hardly know what I figured to myself was served by this, but I meant that if any came looking for me, these were my words to them, and so Farewell.

So in a while I had got a few pounds together, and I went back to the town where I had worked at piecening cotton when a boy, and I asked after a girl I had worked with, and was told she was living there yet, and not married. So then I asked after her dwelling. And it was Mischief-Night when I came there, when the young men go up and down, leaving tokens on doorsteps, and making a racket about. So on my Lucy's door I put a holly bush, which is to say, one loved in secret, and a sprig of birch, which is to say, a pretty wench. Then I stood over in a doorway, and saw my Lucy come and take them. And when she took them I spoke to her. I thought she might not like to wed a cripple, but she never minded it. So we married three days after in the Methodist Chapel, and have had ten children of whom four is living, and two has families of their own. We have been in sore trouble many times for though I could get money, I had always enough to spend it on, but we have done well enough all told, and never a hard word between us, good times or bad. I work now for John Masters, Printer, and I am his chief hand, and I have a house at the works, wherein I am very well set up. As for our children, none of them have been put to factory work; I would sooner starve first. But my son John is apprenticed here, to John Masters, to be a printer under me, and my daughter Ann is in school, and can teach me, and my son Thomas is a mechanic, and has a wife and three children, and he does very well, and my other son James is in America, and works as a clock-maker in a small way. We have the passage money saved up to go and see him, but John Masters swears he cannot go along without me. ..."

"Oh, Creep," said Christopher, with a deep sigh. "So you was all right, in the end. You managed. You always was tough, considering. ... Good for you!"

And he got up, and ran out into the sunshine, leaving the book open on the desk.

19

Two of them, Christopher and Pauline, were conferring in urgent whispers, on the landing outside the bedroom door.

"Come on, Pauley. I got something to show you."

"Show me now."

"Can't. T'isn't here. We gotta go and find it."

"Mam says I'm not to go ramping around with you no more. She says it's your fault we got lost that time."

"We weren't lost, Pauley. We'd 've made it home later."

"Well, what is it then?"

"A message. For us. From Creep. He put it somewhere. We gotta find it."

"There wasn't never any Creep.... You're nutty, that's what. You eff off and leave me be!"

"It's all right, Pauley. Do listen. I know why you don't want to think about him. It's too bad to think about. But it's all right. He didn't come to no harm ... well, he come to harm, but was all right in the end, see, quite all right, and he says he left a message on a bridge....Oh, do let's go, Pauley, I want to find it!"

"What do you mean, *he says*? He never hardly said

nothing...." She stopped.

"There you are," he said, accepting her admission. "I found him, Pauley, sort of. Do *come*. I'll buy you some popcorn soon as I get my pocket money back."

He took her hand, and began to bring her half by force down the stairs. They were narrow, lined with dirty wallpaper. An even narrower passage led back, past Creep's cupboard, to the scullery. The cupboard door was covered over with pasted-on newspapers these days, to keep out the draught from the hole in the wall the demolishers had made. The Council were going to move them out soon, maybe. A clink of dishes in the sink warned Christopher against trying to get Pauline out that way; instead he gently opened the front door.

There was a lady on the step. Dressed posh, coat with brooch on collar, holding gloves. Christopher pulled the door to softly behind him. The lady was looking distressed.

"Christopher!" she said. "Just who I wanted to see. I'm sorry I didn't believe you, dear. But you see we've found your brother's birth certificate now, and we know you were telling the truth. Now, will you tell me what happened to your brother?"

"What brother?" said Christopher, looking back at her with blank eyes. "I never had a brother."

"That isn't what you told me when we talked before," she said gently.

"It's what *you* said," he said stubbornly.

"You must tell me as quick as you can," she said. "He may be in danger, and we have to find him and help him. What happened to him?"

"He's dead," said Christopher. "You'll see. You ask all the neighbours if they ever saw him, they'll tell you

153

no. You've got Pauline telling you no, any time you like to ask."

"I'm asking *you*, Christopher, please!"

"You see," he said, "it's too late. Any brother that I ever had's been dead long ago, long before I was born, or you was, or even our mam. You sherlock round all you like, you won't find him. And I gotta go now."

"Won't you just wait while I talk to your mother?" she said. But Christopher caught Pauline's eye, and they jumped off the doorstep sideways, and ran.

They thought they heard her start her car, as if to come after them driving, but they pushed the loose boarding behind the posters on the fence round the Place, and slipped through, safely, off the road, and out of sight.

But the Place was not, as always till now, deserted. It was bathed in sunlight. The white-washed wall at the far side of it was filthy with fresh writings scribbled over the ghosts of older ones. A lean young man in jeans was standing in the middle of the Place, addressing a dozen others, some of whom had notebooks.

Christopher and Pauline ducked down immediately, and crept into the shelter of the nearest rusting car. The young man's voice reached them.

"It doesn't look much, does it? And yet this is the site of one of the oldest industries in town. The canal you can see there brought coal, and carried away finished goods."

Christopher nudged Pauline, and they fled together across a gap between one car and another.

"Those round declivities you can see," said the voice, "are early blast furnaces. See if you can find traces of a greeny, glassy substance adhering to the brickwork;

that's slag—molten limestone, added to the furnace as a flux for impurities."

Christopher bobbed up, to see how they could get round the intruders. Then, taking Pauline's hand, he rushed her across a rise in the ground, and they slithered down out of sight in a filthy hole.

"If you walk round and look about you," the voice floated over their heads. "You might find evidence of the products of the foundry and its associated industries. ..."

Footsteps. Creeping up the side of the pit, putting his head out, Christopher saw the strangers crawling all over the dump, in ones and twos, and no likely way through them unseen to the canal bank. He ducked back quickly as the teacher and one of the note-takers came towards him. They stood right above Pauline on the rim of the pit, lighting cigarettes in the wind-shadow of a pile of oil-drums. Pauline was all right, really. She might be a pain, but she had commonsense. She didn't panic, and she didn't make a sound, just shrank back into the shadow as far as she could.

Voices. "It did make a mess, sir, didn't it?"

"What did? Ironfounding?"

"The whole thing. The Industrial Revolution. All this muck on the landscape."

"Muck wasn't the worst of it," said the other voice. "But it's our bread-and-butter, isn't it? Any working man would tell you not to quarrel with it. We must come to terms with it somehow. Anybody found anything?" he called.

"Oh, bloody hell!" said Christopher, between clenched teeth. "When are they going to bugger off, and let us get on!" And he scrambled up out of the pit, and stood recklessly in full view.

The strangers were converging upon the teacher. And coming towards him also was an old man, a tramp, with his coat tied up with string. His face was brown and cracked as old wood, but the eyes in it were pale—a bright pale rainlit grey.

He held out to the teacher a handful of rusty iron, and said, "Like this was it, you was wanting?"

Christopher stood unnoticed. He beckoned Pauline to come up and join him.

"Oh, yes, look, hand-made. You can see they're different from modern machine-made nails....Look everybody! And think, these were probably forge-made by little children standing on boxes to reach the hearth."

"Thank God nothing like that happens now!" someone said.

From behind the speaker the two children suddenly skipped round the group and ran for it, haring over the dirt and rubbish, and racing for the canal path. Reaching it, they looked back, and saw that nobody was following them. They slowed up, breathless, and Christopher took Pauline's hand.

"Is it far, Chris?" she said, looking mutinous.

"Maybe. He said he came back as far as he could remember, and I don't know how far that was. But don't fret, Pauley. We'll go slow. And it's nice out there, remember?"

And when they reached it, it was. They passed by the dirt and soot-grimed derelict piles of the centre of town, and the wire-fenced, bleak clean new factories, and the back gardens of hundreds of little houses, and came into open fields. The spring freshness had gone from the land, and spreads of dark dusty green leaves broke the sun into fragments, and mottled the path.

The cool surface of the cut was broken by drifts of arrow-head, with its tiny bruised white flowers; the rambling rose spread arcs of fragile pink petalled flowers in the hedge. They saw a kingfisher, just as they reached the junction, leaving his perch at the waterline, and skimming brilliantly along the cloud-filled water. They pulled thick grasses, and chewed the juicy ends. Beyond one bridge they disturbed a heron. It looked slender and dignified poised on the bank, but suddenly large and clumsy flapping away.

By and by they came again to the bridge where *CREEP* was written. It was still there; Christopher had not dreamed it. He stared at it, and then, on impulse, pulled a stick from the hedgerow and beat at the tall nettles that grew thick and high almost up to the word *CREEP*, masking the lower stones from view. And then, vigorously, he trampled them down, thrust them aside.

"Look, Pauley!" he said.

He had uncovered, below the stone which said *CREEP*, another, inscribed in a different style. This one had been cut in small, regular, neat letters, with serifs and triangular grooves, like the letters on tombstones.

"I told you it'd be here," said Christopher.

"What does it say?" she asked.

He read to her:

> "TIME AS IT IS CANNOT STAY,
> NOR AS IT WAS CANNOT BE
> DISSOLVING AND PASSING AWAY
> ARE THE WORLD, THE AGES AND ME."

"What does it mean?" asked Pauline.

Christopher was frowning at the letters, committing them to memory. "What he *said* he meant by it," he told her, "was that these are his words to us, and so Farewell."

Author's Note

I have acquired many debts of gratitude to people who gave me help in research for this book. To Mr Forshaw of Northern Spinners, Ltd, Mr Watt of Bilsthorpe Colliery, and Mr Brown of Isleworth Foundry for invaluable help in understanding and interpreting the historical and technical background; to Miss Elisabeth Reisch who by relieving me of other responsibilities made time available to me in which to write this book; to my family, and to John Townsend and his family, my companions cruising the canal system, my thanks are particularly due.

The book was written during my tenure of an Arts Council Fellowship at Brighton Polytechnic.

Also by Jill Paton Walsh

THE DOLPHIN CROSSING

The story of two boys and the friendship between them during the early days of the Second World War - Pat and John both knew the risks they were running yet took a boat to help save the stranded British army from Dunkirk.

FIREWEED

A hauntingly realistic story of a pair of runaways alone in London and hiding from the authorities during the terrifying Blitz of 1940.

A PARCEL OF PATTERNS
(*Puffin Plus   for older readers*)

The plague comes to the village of Eyam, possibly brought by a parcel of dress patterns from London. The villagers make a vow to contain the plague within their own boundaries, which forces Mall to make her own heartbreaking decision. She must not go to meet her beloved Thomas for fear of passing the sickness on to him   but how can she bear not to see him, or at least to tell him how she is? This stunningly written novel is a powerful drama and a moving love story.